Tomorrow

Tomorrow

Lou Berry

Second printing

This is a work of fiction. All names, characters, and incidents are either products of the author's imagination or are used fictitiously. No reference to any real person or event is intended or should be inferred.

PUBLISHED BY D-PI PUBLICATIONS
Nashville, Tennessee 37216

Library of Congress Catalog Card No: 94-60123
ISBN: 1-55523-681-2

Printed in the United States of America

This book is dedicated to those who may be experiencing the pain of divorce or turmoil in their relationships.
Keep hope and remember that in time this too will pass.

Tomorrow, and tomorrow, and tomorrow,
Creeps in this petty pace from day to day,
To the last syllable of recorded time;
And all our yesterdays have lighted fools
The way to dusty death. Out, out, brief candle!
Life's but a walking shadow, a poor player
That struts and frets his hour upon the stage,
And then is heard no more.

—Shakespeare, *Macbeth, V, v*

Acknowledgments

For unending support I would first like to thank my higher power.
Thanks also to my family, Carolyn, Carol, Eunice, Barbara, Charles,
Eric, Rosie, and Krystal. Special thanks also to the man in my life
for being there for me and for making valuable suggestions for this book,
including the title. Thanks to my friends, Lynda, Elise, Earline, Benita,
Glen, and Larry from the *Washington Times*. Thanks to my coworkers,
Edward, Rhonda, Shirley, Reggie, Joann, Laquanda, Veda, Pat, Gary,
Jena, and Edwin, and also to the Harvest Dinner speakers,
Valerie and Renée. Thanks to my photographer, Nasir. And lastly,
a special thanks to Winston-Derek Publishers Group, Inc.
for allowing me the opportunity to become a published author.

Chapter One: January

January 1
Friday, 1:30 A.M.

I can still hear firecrackers and gunshots popping in the night as the people continue to celebrate the New Year. I am not sleepy, and I am not tired. I guess I am still wired up over what happened to me earlier.

I went out earlier during the evening, and when I returned I put my key in the lock and turned it swiftly. All I could think about was getting inside out of the cold and finding something to eat. I was going to head straight for the refrigerator, but as soon as I stepped inside my apartment, a man came up behind me and put his gloved hand over my mouth. I could not see him, even from the corner of my eye. The only thing I knew about him was that he was strong. He put tape over my mouth, blindfolded me, and tied my hands behind my back. I was so frightened I nearly pissed on the floor. This man did not talk to me while he did this. He just moved swiftly and efficiently.

After he rendered me helpless, he led me to the bedroom and pushed me down on the bed. I had been cold a few minutes earlier, but now I was burning up, with beads of perspiration swelling up on my forehead. My legs started to shake, and they felt like jelly as he straddled them and tied each one to a bedpost. He pushed my dress up and ran his fingers up and down my thighs for about ten minutes. Then I heard a noise like he was taking something out of his pocket, and then there was a clicking sound. My heart nearly stopped, because I just knew he had a switchblade. I soon felt the sharp edges of a knife moving softly up and down my thighs and legs, and then the blade caught the rim of my panties. He ripped the seams on each side and jerked them off. By now my dress was over my head. I didn't know what he was going to do next, but I could feel him staring at me and examining my private parts. For a few seconds there was complete silence, and then he left the room. I listened to the strangely familiar sound of his footsteps as he moved in the hallway. He went into the kitchen, and I heard him open the refrigerator. I sighed as he came back into the room, because by now I knew who he was.

He stood quietly for a minute, then suddenly I felt his hands and then his finger, fingerfucking me. He was not rough as he moved his finger rhythmically for about five minutes. Then, with his bare hands, he ripped the front of my dress open. I felt the cold knife blade on my chest and then between my breasts as he cut my bra open. He sucked my breasts tenderly for a few minutes, and then he rubbed something very cold and wet up and down my leg. It was ice, and it felt weird. Then he took that little piece of ice and stuck it where he had just fingerfucked me, and I moaned. Then I felt his tongue licking the inside of my thighs and then licking and sucking at the piece of ice. When the ice was totally melted, he raised up and spoke for the first time. He said, "Happy New Year," and he asked me if I wanted to come. He took the blindfold and tape off. Finally my hands were free, and I slapped him very hard across the face. It was my husband, Mark. He nearly scared the living shit out of me, and to him this was exciting. So now, even though we drank two bottles of wine celebrating the New Year, I am still wired, while Mark is sleeping like an angel right here beside me. I will never forget this shit.

January 4
Monday, Midnight

The temperature outside dropped, and the television weatherman has predicted freezing rain before morning. Right now my sinuses feel stopped up because the heat in this apartment is very dry. I usually keep the thermostat on high; otherwise it will get too cool. This apartment is not insulated very well, and air comes in around the windows and under the door.

I know I must look strange with Noxema caked on my face, my hair in curlers, and me wearing this old gray flannel gown. This gown is ragged as hell; the seams under the arms are pretty ripped, and the hemline is uneven, but it's comfortable. Besides, Mark is not here; he's in Houston. So why should I dress up in a lacy nightgown?

Speaking of Mark, this is the time of the year when I reminisce about when we first met at a New Year's Eve Party. We were introduced by Mattie Thomas, a good friend and my coworker at the time. Mark was the disc jockey at the party and very much the center of attention. He was wearing a maroon suit and a pale pink shirt, and I figured any man bold enough to wear an outfit so colorful must be loaded with personality. Mattie knew Mark personally, as she did most of the people at the party. While she moved around the room socializing with old friends, I sat at the table with Roy, Mattie's old man. It was obvious that he was just as lost as I was. He didn't know any of those people, either. Mattie made her rounds and returned to the table. She said in a low voice, "The D.J., Mark Williams, wants to meet you." I immediately turned and looked in his direction and then felt Mattie's hand gripping mine as she led the way to his table.

He was an attractive bronze color and had a neatly trimmed afro haircut. He had almond-shaped eyes and a thin moustache. Mark looked to be about five feet ten inches tall, and I thought he probably weighed about one hundred and ninety pounds. He had a muscular build like someone who lifted weights and worked out. Mattie introduced us, and Mark took the lead. He turned out to be quite a talker, and I stayed with him behind the counter for the remainder of the party, talking to him between his record spinning. When he asked me, I gave him my telephone number and address. Then I left with Mattie and Roy at around 2 A.M.

Mark called me the next day, and the rest is history. We used to sit and talk for hours. Sometimes we would just sit in the car and listen to the radio and laugh and talk. He was a drywall subcontractor, a part-time disc jockey, a fisherman, a self-taught auto mechanic, a motorcycle rider, a chess-player, a weight lifter, and a ladies' man. I found out about that last one on my own. He was a charming person when he wanted to be, but sometimes he would become very moody. Overall, Mark really liked to have fun, and he loved excitement. During the beginning of our courtship, he aggressively pursued me. But when he felt he had won me over, he started to act sort of cool. Of course by now I could not get enough of him, and I started to push the issue of marriage.

Five years ago we got married. Mattie Thomas, the friend that introduced us, was surprised. She said, "Girl, I was thinking that he would be somebody for you to fuck off with, not get married to!" I had some family and other friends who were not happy about this wedding, and they told me they thought we were too different. They seemed most troubled by his carefree attitude about women and by his reputation of being a ladies' man. Valerie, one of my very dear friends, told me that this kind of thing brings nothing but heartache.

I was a social worker at a local mental health facility, and when I married Mark I was doing well financially. As a matter of fact, I had just paid off my car and did not have any debts. I had an unrealistic picture of married life, though, because I really believed that we would be so happy every day. I thought going to bed whenever we liked and just being together would be like heaven on earth. I really think most young women idealize marriage and have unrealistic expectations. What I have learned is that marriage is great when everything is going your way, but just have a problem or a crisis, and it becomes hell. The bottom line is that marriage is something you have to work at, and a marriage is not going to be good simply because that is what you want. Both people have to work seriously toward harmony.

I think couples should have to attend marriage classes and take tests and make a score of one hundred on every test before even considering tying the nuptial knot. I really feel that there are some things everyone should know, practice, and be responsible for prior to marriage. They are—just to name a few—1) loyalty—being committed to the relationship, and I mean deciding to give up all the old girlfriends and all the old boyfriends, concentrating on each other, learning the things that make each other happy, and putting all this to practice. 2) There should be some focus, some set of goals for the marriage. The couple should be trying to accomplish something together that they could not do otherwise, and they should be unified on these goals. 3) Each person should be a productive, contributing member of society—in other words, hold down a legal job. 4) Childrearing is the most important job a couple will ever have. As parents, both parties are responsible for shaping and molding the child and ensuring that he or she becomes a productive, contributing member of society. When you have children, your life ceases to be your own. From that point on, you will share and have to think about what effect your behavior, actions, or decisions will have on that child. Parents definitely should not be selfish individuals. 5) Know how to get along with your in-laws, and why this is important. In-laws are family, and they do have influence. Most people care about and love their mothers and fathers, so dogging your mother-in-law is only going to alienate you further from your spouse. Plus, if you have children from this union, then these in-laws are your children's blood kin. 6) Budgeting and paying bills. This is something that both people need to know how to do so that if one becomes ill, goes crazy, gets incarcerated, dies, or just leaves because they don't want to be bothered, the other one is not totally ignorant of the couple's financial situation. 7) Running a household. Both people should know how to cook, clean, cut grass, and change diapers. I feel like these seven things are just the basics and are the foundation to a good marriage.

Getting back to my marriage, two weeks of married life, and it was obvious that marriage was not all lovemaking and games. See, if we had been required to take a *test,* I would have known some of this shit beforehand. Mark suddenly became helpless—he completely forgot how to do the laundry and how to prepare breakfast. Tasks he had once managed with ease as a bachelor were now a major ordeal.

My work hours vary, and Mark had problems adjusting to my work schedule, especially because dinner was served at different times every day. Not to mention the fact that he would usually get home before I would, and he'd still be waiting for me to come in and prepare dinner.

After six months of marriage and living in Mark's bachelor's apartment with girlie pictures on the wall, I started to look for a house and talked daily about buying one. It took me three months to talk Mark into buying a house, and when we closed on the house, I could tell he was frightened. I guess the commitment to pay for a house is probably the biggest financial obligation a person will ever make, and he was scared. It showed in his face. But I suppose for a man who had never even had a checking account until he got married, he wasn't doing too badly. I can't imagine going to each place of business to pay my bills in cash, but Mark did. He used to carry large sums of cash on him all the time. In any event, we moved into that three-bedroom house in the northeast section of town and then did what a lot of people do—we acquired debt and more debt.

Mark told me he had *allowed* me to get a house, and now he wanted a new van. He acted as though it was a contest—"Let's Make A Deal," or some such game. I bought some furniture, and Mark bought a motorcycle. I got a washer and dryer, and Mark got a new stereo system with speakers, tape deck, and dance lights. We got all this stuff on credit, and the credit never seemed to end. It just went on and on. But I'm getting sleepy now. It's almost 1:00 A.M., and I can see through the window that snowflakes are falling. I have to go to work tomorrow, if I can drive under these weather conditions.

January 5
Tuesday, 10:00 P.M.

The weather was simply awful today. We don't usually have winters this harsh. I mean, I got really scared driving in the snow. I got stuck at least five times, and I was glad I left work early. I saw several cars slide off the road. The interstate was unreal. Cars were abandoned in the middle of the highway. I really don't know how I made it home, because I'm a nervous driver, anyway. But I did get home, and I will take tomorrow off if the conditions are like today.

I was exhausted when I got home, so I took a nap and ended up sleeping until nine. Now that I'm up, I think I'll pack some of my clothes and linens. I have a few boxes stacked in the corner of my bedroom. Georgia Haynes, a coworker, offered her assistance last week. She said, "Girl, listen, if you need any help packing, let me know, and I'll help you."

Georgia is tall and thin with fair skin and green eyes. Her hair is dark brown, and her curls are tight afro-curls. She's a nurse practitioner, and she's smart and quick as a whip. I told her that I appreciated her offer, but that I have everything under control.

Georgia Haynes has such a way of categorizing people, and sometimes it makes me uncomfortable. She has probably put all of her friends and coworkers in some psychological category. She labeled Nettie the ward clerk as a borderline schizophrenic, Dave the administrative assistant as neurotic, and Marvin, one of the clinical psychologists, as a latent homosexual.

When I think back to the time Georgia met Mark, I remember that she later whispered to me that he has sociopathic tendencies. Although she never told me directly, she hinted that I have hysterical tendencies. It was Georgia who said to me a month ago, "Norma, I may be speaking out of order, but you shouldn't quit your job and follow that sociopath anywhere."

Well, I responded by saying, "That *sociopath* just happens to be my husband, Georgia."

I suppose guilt made her offer her assistance with my packing. But you know, I really do have an uneasy feeling about packing up and moving across the country with Mark. Sometimes I am almost one hundred percent positive that Georgia is right, and then those feelings fade and I am one hundred percent sure that I am doing the right thing. Hell, I hope it is the right thing.

January 6
Wednesday, 8:00 P.M.

Mark is the only man that I have ever been with sexually who knows how to really turn me on. I had four lovers before Mark, and I enjoyed sex, but I never reached orgasm. I will never forget the first time we were intimate. It was about two months after we met. I had prepared a meal and invited him over. He arrived on time with a bottle of wine. We drank a couple of glasses before dinner, and I guess Mark got hot and bothered, because he came up behind me as I put the glasses in the sink, held my waist with both hands, and sniffed at my neck and ears. Then he turned me where we were facing each other, and he rubbed my nose and licked my face. This sensation was different, and I smiled, which gave him encouragement. The next thing I knew, I was lying on top of the kitchen table, and Mark was standing over me, smiling. He reached his hand under my dress and pulled my panties off slowly and sniffed them. Then he put his hand between my legs and sniffed at my neck. I was melting, so he pulled me up, and we got on the floor. Mark tried a couple of positions, but when he penetrated me from behind and made those fast jerking movements that were just right, to my surprise, when Mark found himself riding a cloud, so was I. It nearly scared me to death—my legs started to shake, and that sweet good feeling in my loins just took full control, and I said words I did not even know I had in my vocabulary. That was the first time I reached an orgasm. He truly satisfies me, and he knows it. I guess you could say Mark taught me everything I needed to know about sex. It was as if the lovers I had before Mark did not even exist. When we were dating, I was never bored because I never knew what he would try next. I do believe he gets a kick out of keeping me in awe.

January 7
Thursday, 9:00 P.M.

I did not go to work today because last night we got six inches of snow. I guess it's really no big deal about my missing work since I am quitting anyway.

I got some packing done today. Mark and I have already discussed leaving the furniture in storage for a while, so the main things to move are clothes and small household appliances.

I wrote some goodbye notes to give to my patients. Only a few of them know that I'm leaving. I have a present caseload of twenty-six patients. Half of them are suffering with depression, and the other half of them have either personality disorders or schizophrenia—mainly Schizophrenia Chronic Undifferentiated Type. We spend all our lives labeling people, and when we have a problem labeling we find a catch-all. I mean, schizophrenia C.U.T. is really another way of saying we really don't know what to call you, so you must be C.U.T.

I will really miss some of my patients, like Tory, for instance. He is twenty-three years old and has spent most of his life in an institution. He is tall, muscular, and ebony black. Tory frequently has delusions that he is extremely wealthy and that his body changes colors. Sometimes he is white, and sometimes he is rainbow colored.

Then there is Betty, a fifty-year-old white female who was recently brought to the hospital by police after they picked her up at the bus station when she showed signs of confusion and aggression. Initially she was unable to give us any information, not even her name. Staff members checked papers in her purse and found some documents with her name on them. Betty had no inkling where she came from. She just kept repeating that she was on her way to marry Jesus Christ.

One of my very favorite patients is a manic-depressive named Anna. Anna has been in the hospital for about three weeks this time. The other day the ward nurse was passing out medications. Anna looked at the nurse with fire in her eyes and said, "I ain't taking that fucking poison." Then she excited some of the other patients by getting them to dance and sing loudly, and she encouraged them not to take their medication. Anna really got out of hand when she started banging her head against the wall and screaming at the top of her voice. She was put in seclusion and later on when she got out, she wrote the following note:

Staff—

I'm sorry I was on the end of my rope; my physique was marred; my body is dead; my dog is lost and my man is doing without; and today is the first day of the rest of my life. I needed a rest, not rules and regulations, not just to help you control your ward; rules don't apply, nor meet the needs of individuals at certain given situations. I was scorned for getting other people involved, ie., dancing and singing, I was drugged, I refuse to degenerate, Hell, I am not a potato. I just am tuned to the beat of a different drummer. I have some suggestions:

1. Morning exercises to music

2. Exercise classes daily

a) Individuals should be able to leave the grounds for an hour at a time.

b) Emergency—get organized, anything can happen over the weekend.

And she signed it and drew a big butterfly in bright red ink at the bottom of the page.

I have lots of memories here at Hillhaven, and the staff I will not forget, either. One person in particular is Leaidi, an African from Nigeria. He is a psychiatric technician and a very warm, likeable person. He's a senior in college and has been in the states for five years, but he still has problems understanding some English words. I remember once when one of the doctors asked Leaidi if there was Malox on the ward, and Leaidi went into the dayroom and yelled, "Malox! Malox!" I stopped him and explained that Malox is a medicine. He obviously thought Malox was a patient. He was quite embarrassed at first, but we later had a good laugh about it.

We used to have some nice parties at Hillhaven. Every year the staff would have Christmas parties on the grounds. We all knew we were not supposed to have booze on the grounds, and who do you suppose put booze in the punch? None other than the famous medical director, Doctor Smith. He always slipped it in the bowl; it must've been grain alcohol, 'cause the shit always got you when you least expected it. Our Christmas parties were always in the late evenings, and we were encouraged to bring our spouses. Mark would never go with me. As a matter of fact, whenever I asked him to come to the party with me, it usually caused an argument. It took me a long time to figure out that Mark was harboring feelings of inferiority. He did not go to college and felt uneasy around my coworkers. But Mark is very bright—brilliant is a better word; he's very well read and can talk about any subject under the sun.

January 8
Friday, 6:30 A.M.

I did not rest well last night. It is exactly seven days before my last day at work. I am marking the days off on my calendar. Mark should be here on the fifteenth.

It may be a bad time to quit my job, but among other reasons, I feel I need a rest. I feel so tired most of the time, and some days I feel very old. I think the last six or seven months have aged me ten years. Anyway, I will give all my patients their goodbye letters today. They will have at least a week to adjust.

January 8
Friday, 6:30 P.M.

Driving conditions were better today, and I got home at the usual time—five o'clock—but I have barely had time to catch my breath. The telephone was ringing off the hook when I got home, and just as I picked up, they hung up. That is so aggravating.

I got cramps today. I don't always get them, but most of the time I get some warning, such as my breasts getting very sore and swelling, and I get a bloated feeling in my stomach. I stopped taking my birth control pills a year after we married, but nothing has happened yet. I went through the temperature phase where I took my temperature daily and recorded it and tried to figure out the time when I was fertile. After some months of going through that and being disappointed every month because my period would always show like clockwork, I just stopped and simply decided what will be will be.

Oh, before I forget, I met a new worker today—Dr. David Monroe, a tall, muscular, neatly dressed, handsome man. His skin looked black as onyx and smooth as velvet. He has the blackest, prettiest skin I have ever seen, and he was immaculate; everything he had on matched to perfection. He stood there and had an air about him, like no matter what challenge you posed he could overcome it. He could easily have been a black prince. He will be doing some emergency calls here. The nurse on the unit introduced us, but before she did I honest to God could feel him staring at me. After she introduced us, he spoke pleasantly and acted like he wanted to say something else but did not.

Anyway, Georgia Haynes was her usual self, profiling the man before she really knew him. "He is an obsessive-compulsive type—perfectionist is probably a better term. Just look at him walking around here like he knows everything, like he has the answer to the answer," she said after Dr. Monroe passed us in the lobby. Lord, there's no help for Georgia—she is almost forty and has never married, she can't seem to stay in a relationship longer than a couple of months, and is there any wonder why? What man in his right mind would want to listen to her recall all the diagnoses in the DSM IV as she labels her friends, coworkers, and then his family and friends one by one? Georgia loves to talk about her business and other people's business. I swear she is like an old refrigerator—she can't keep anything. Why do I remain friends with Georgia? Well, I really think she means well most of the time.

January 9
Saturday, 1:00 P.M.

For some strange reason I woke up early this morning, I think around 6:00, and for Saturday that is unusual for me. It may have been a dream that woke me, but I can't remember any of it.

Anyway, I miss Mark, and if I didn't write in this journal every day I would probably be nuts. I wonder if Mark misses me? It's hard to know, because Mark is so strange sometimes, and I know why he is that way. His father died when Mark was four years old, and his mother was left to rear six children alone, and she was not stable. As a matter of fact, she went totally bananas a year after Mark's father died. One day she decided she was going to clean house, and she put her children out of the house and would not allow them to come back inside. After that incident the children were split up and reared by various relatives. Those were bad years for Mark. He used to talk about never getting enough to eat and how no one seemed to care what time he came home or even if he came home at all. All of this has had its effects on Mark. I love the man, but sometimes I think my love frightens him to death. And just when I think everything is fine between us, sometimes he'll do something to anger or alienate me.

I suppose I have answered my own question; that's the anxiety I'm feeling. Now that I have made all these plans, will something happen to deter them? I guess time will tell.

January 9
Saturday, 5:00 P.M.

I had an unusual experience after my earlier entry. I got my mail, and the telephone bill was included among four letters. I opened the phone bill and it totaled $75. Well, that did not alarm me, because Mark and I have talked a lot over the holidays, especially now that he returned to Texas. But there were two strange calls billed to my number. The calls were made from Houston, Texas to Knoxville and were billed to this number. This Knoxville number is not familiar to me at all. The calls totaled $28.00. They had to have been calls Mark made, but why did he bill them to this number? They're probably business calls. Maybe I should dial the number and find out, but what on earth will I say? "Hello, I'm Norma Jean Williams, and my telephone bill has calls on it with your number." That sounds stupid as hell. I have to think some more about it.

What I really need to do is make a list of things I need to get done next week like, 1) get change of address cards, 2) take old clothes to Goodwill, and 3) notify the phone company to terminate service.

My body is giving me signals that I need to eat. I have only had one hard boiled egg the entire day. I really need to work on my eating habits. One day I eat all day long, and the next day it's like I'm fasting, only I don't plan it that way, it just happens. That's one of the reasons I only weigh 105 pounds, aside from smoking two packs of cigarettes per day.

When I married Mark I only weighed one hundred pounds, so I have gained five pounds. Yes, I was a short, thin, frail bride. I take after my father's people. In fact, I look just like my father's mother. She was a thin, frail, short, dainty little person with light baked-brown skin and long, thick, ebony-black, coarse hair. My father often used to look at me, shake his head, and then say, "This child sure look like Mama."

It's strange in a way how family members share the same blood ties, the same genes. A member of the family may die, yet they live on because their children live and have children with similar genetic make-up. Perhaps that is why I want children so bad—I want to know that I have not just passed this way and then perished forever but will live even when I am dead and gone.

I really have to get something to eat because my stomach is damn near singing a song, it is growling so strong.

January 10
Sunday, 10:00 A.M.

I have eaten a delicious breakfast of pancakes, eggs, bacon, juice, the works. I had planned to attend church services, but I am just too full. All I can do is lie here and write. I was just thinking about Mama, Daddy, my sister Janie Mae, and my brother Sam.

My parents married young—Mama was seventeen and Daddy was nineteen. Mama was pregnant when they married, because they married in November and Janie Mae and Sam were born in July the next year. It was ten years later before I was born. As a matter of fact, Mama was beginning to think she could not have any more children, and then at age twenty-seven it happened again.

Having a sister and brother ten years older than me was a lonely feeling. I mean, we didn't grow up together, but we're close now. I sort of looked at Janie Mae as a mother figure. Janie Mae was smart and a tough act to follow in school. That girl got straight A's in biology and chemistry. The teachers used to look at me with disgust because I just wasn't that smart in the sciences. Janie Mae with all those brains ended up doing the same thing in a way that Mama did: she fell in love, got pregnant, got married, and had the baby eight months later. Janie Mae and her husband James are still together. They both work at a local shoe factory, and they have five children. All those straight A's gone down the drain. My Mama used to encourage Janie Mae to go on to college, but her husband would do something to sabotage it every time.

Getting back to Mama, she brought us up to go to church services, Baptist Training Union, and choir rehearsal. The entire sabbath day was spent in church.

Daddy used to read passages from the Bible, but he did not attend church services often. This used to piss Mama off, and they'd argue about it every Sunday. Eventually she mellowed out and didn't seem to let it bother her.

In the early days, I remember a wood stove stuffed full with wood and burning so fiercely that parts of the stovepipe were actually red with heat on winter mornings. I can vaguely remember that we had an outhouse, because I was afraid of the spiders in it. Anyway, on Sundays Mama would cook tenderloin, gravy, rice, and biscuits for breakfast, and then we would eat and be off to church.

Mama was a short, light-brown-skinned woman with a heart-shaped face, big brown eyes, high cheekbones, and long black hair that she wore twisted in a knot on the top of her head most of the time.

I bet Mama is getting dressed for church right this minute. She has been living alone since Daddy died five years ago, but she keeps active with her quilting, gardening, knitting, and other hobbies.

I used to call home every Sunday to chat, but I am trying to conserve, so I don't call as often.

Mama didn't say too much when I told her I was moving to Houston. She got real quiet for a few minutes, and then she said, "Child, if you need me for anything, don't you hesitate to call your

Mama." Yeah, there's nothing better than a Mama who cares about her child.

January 11
Monday, 6:06 P.M.

Work was bearable, but the weather is turning bad again with rain and sleet. The weatherman predicted a drop in temperature and possibly an ice storm. There are thin patches and sheets of ice formed on the highway now.

This is eerie—it feels like an omen, like maybe this move is not the right thing to do now. I know I should have my head examined for trying to move during the winter, but do I really have a choice? Why should I move and leave my job of five years and my friends? Let's see, let me count the reasons:

1. Mark and I have been living apart for nearly a year. Work got slow here in Knoxville, and he got more opportunities in Texas. They are building hospitals, shopping malls, and business buildings. We see each other about once a month, which is not enough.

2. It is economically necessary. We can't continue to operate two households much longer. Besides, I already had to put our house up for sale and move in this small apartment to save money.

3. The third and final reason is because the IRS has been really messing with me, telling me they are going to take half my paycheck because we owe them. For two of the years we filed, Mark did not have enough income tax withheld, and now we have to pay. If they take half my check per month, I will have to quit work, because I will not be able to afford to live in this apartment. Anyway, I am tired of this shit. I mean, we're both working, trying to make it, and they take a hell of a lot of money out of my check. Now they're giving me hell about more money, and I can't take too much more of this. I mean, I don't mind paying my fair share, but they need to be reasonable. If they take so much money from me that I can't afford to live in the

style to which I have become accustomed, then it will just make more sense for me to become unemployed. I wonder if they mess with the big corporations like that, the people who really have big bucks. I don't see why they just don't take out the appropriate amount of money during the year and just do away with income taxes. Anyway, enough of that shit, it's depressing.

My friend Valerie Davis called this afternoon. We grew up together and went to college together. Valerie married Jack Davis shortly after graduation and started her family. Jack is a good man and a hard worker. He works at a local cabinet factory. Valerie has never really worked a job in her profession. She has a degree in accounting but has no experience. Jack doesn't push her either; he just lets her move at her own speed, so she does as she pleases. They have two girls, and they are adorable. Valerie is now selling home arts and crafts and will be having a show on Friday night. She made me promise I would attend.

Now I guess I will get me a hot bath, wash my hair, and do my nails.

January 12
Tuesday, 10:00 P.M.

I am tired as hell. On the way to work, the ice-covered streets made my car slip and slide. I nearly had an accident. Several people called in today, but Georgia showed. We had a Treatment Team meeting, if you can call three people a Treatment Team.

I reviewed each of my cases and then wrote updated progress notes for the new worker who will be taking my position in another two weeks.

I cleaned out my desk drawers, cleared the file cabinet, and then took my pictures from the walls in my office. Well, at least it will be my office until Friday.

The reality of leaving this place, this city, is now finally sinking in and frightening the hell out of me. But you know, I had to smile to myself, thinking about my anxiety about leaving Hillhaven. How many times have my patients expressed their separation anxiety to me? Only today during that period of packing and clearing away my things did I feel I could truly empathize with them.

It is frightening to leave the familiar and go to a world of unknowns, where people have faces but no names until you meet them and get to know them.

Something unexpected happened this evening at 7:00. Mark called and said the weather was bad in Houston. He said they were having an ice storm and it might be too bad for him to get here by Friday. He ended the conversation by saying he would come here as soon as he could. Surprisingly, I did not panic. I will go on with my termination as planned. I will take it day by day, step by step.

January 13
Wednesday, 10:00 P.M.

I had a shocking day at work. I went on the unit at 3:00 P.M. At the change of shift, the day nurse signaled for quiet from the staff, because she was ready to give her report. They were all seated around a table with white uniforms on, listening intently as she reviewed each individual patient. Everybody was doing fairly well, except the new admission that came in early this morning. She was a thirty-two-year-old black female, severely depressed. She overdosed on two hundred aspirins and cut her wrist with a razor blade. She refused to talk to anyone and just cried frequently. Well, I decided I would meet this poor soul and try and persuade her to talk. I went in her room, and I seated myself in a chair next to her bed. The bed had a covered-up lifeless lump in it. "Have you eaten?" I asked. Of course I got no reply, so I continued to talk about the weather, about food, clothes, shopping. I just rattled on and on until I heard a low voice ask, "Do you have children?"

I said, "No, I don't, but I love children and hope to have some one day."

The woman in the bed started to cry and mumbled, "I had a baby, and it died from crib death, and I had to have a hysterectomy four months after that, so I cannot have any more children." All the while her head was under the covers as she talked.

I said to her, "Please look at me, I want to tell you something, I promise I will not bite." The woman still would not uncover her head. "It's not the end of the world," I said.

This statement elicited a response. "How would you know? You're just a lousy social worker."

I said, "It's okay for you to be angry, you just go right ahead and get it all out. I will be right here for you." I think that moved her, because she removed the covers from her face and looked me dead in the eyes. Well, there was something awfully familiar about those eyes and that smile that I saw gradually spreading across her face. This was not April Fool, and this was no joke; this was Rachel Bass, only she was not a Bass now because she was married. I went to college with this girl. I hadn't seen her in years. We hugged each other, and I said, "Rachel, the last time I talked to you, you were heading to medical school."

She said, "Norma Jean, Girl, medical school was a real *bitch!* Pressure cooker is probably the best description. You just would not believe the demands put on you in medical school, the long hours of studying, the seminars, the favoritism, criticism, nepotism, need I say more? It was just shitty, but I had a difficult time giving it up, 'cause you know my mother always discouraged the idea of my being a doctor. But finally I knew I was tired of the shit, hell, I didn't know if I was going or coming, so after a year and a half of medical school, I quit and married another student—he's now an anesthesiologist. I have worked a dozen part-time jobs, I sat on half a dozen boards, I have traveled until I was bored. Then I wanted a baby, and it took me several months to get pregnant, and when that baby girl was born I knew she was my salvation, my purpose in life. I loved her so much, and then two weeks later she died mysteriously of crib death. To add insult to injury, I had tumors in my womb and had to have a complete hysterectomy. Now that was the ultimate. I really felt things were coming apart by the seams right before my very eyes, and I wanted out, I did not want to face another day of this shit, so I made an attempt on my life. My husband found me, and the emergency room staff sent me here on emergency papers against my will because they felt I was a danger to myself. I will never try any stupid ass shit like this again." A nurse came in with an antidepressant pill, and Rachel swallowed it with no problem.

I told Rachel there are an awful lot of children out there that could use a good home and a lot of love, especially handicapped children. Her eyes lit up. I hugged her and she whispered, "Thank you."

I later asked Georgia to check up on Rachel, since I knew I would be leaving in a few days.

January 14
Thursday, 8:00 P.M.

I almost lost my cool at work today when my coworkers began to ask me when was I leaving, because I don't know what is going to happen. Tomorrow is the big day; I guess I'll have to wear a mask the entire day.

January 15
Friday, 1:00 A.M.

I was asleep, and someone called here about fifteen minutes ago and held the telephone, never said a word. I hung up. Somebody being cute, a teenager probably. I hate shit like that with a passion.

January 15
Friday, 11:30 p.m.

I may be a dedicated worker, but one thing I am not is on time. But this morning I was at work ten minutes early. I had an impulse once today to cancel my resignation.

The "farewell party" had been planned, and my coworkers came in to work carrying covered dishes and brown paper sacks filled with goodies that smelled sweet and tasty.

The dinner party was set up in the conference room. They had a long table with a white embroidered tablecloth and a beautiful floral centerpiece. There were banners on the wall in aqua-green, my favorite color, that read "Good Luck Norma Jean."

It was Georgia who presented the farewell gift, a beautiful brass magazine holder. It took every ounce of my strength to keep from crying as I stood and thanked them and asked them to pray for me and Mark.

Georgia sat next to me, and I have never heard her sound sad, but she said, "I am going to miss you. Good luck."

Mrs. Wilson, a middle-aged woman, sat at the side of the table. Mrs. Wilson is such a sweet person. She usually brought diet foods for lunch, but most of the time she would eat a Snickers bar after eating the diet food. She commented on the tasty food and then guiltily said, "I must not eat desert."

Coffee Tanner, a slim, blond white woman was standing near the punch bowl filling her paper cup with frappe. Her name sure doesn't fit her. I thought Coffee was a snob when I first started to work at Hillhaven. She had such an aristocratic air about her. After the first year, I learned a lot about Coffee, and she is really a very nice person.

George Carter, a small-framed white man with black hair and a smooth, soft-looking face came behind me and hugged me. He has the cutest little boy face, and his gestures and movements are very effeminate. It is no secret George is gay and has lived with another man for years. I smiled when I thought about it, but George's homosexual relationship has lasted a lot longer than some traditional marriages and relationships.

George has been at Hillhaven for about fifteen years now. He is a psychiatric nurse, and he is damn good. He walked over to the punch bowl and greeted Marvin Tate. They talked for a few minutes. Georgia hunched me in the side; she wanted me to notice them together. She has always said that Marvin is a latent homosexual. I really don't feel I can draw any accurate conclusions from the two of them standing there talking. It's no big deal. Besides, Marvin is married and has three children. I know some married people exhibit homosexual behaviors; I guess that would make them bisexual. I just find it difficult to believe that Marvin would be interested in another man. He just doesn't fit that profile.

Anita, my supervisor, was giggling and talking with two or three people. She was a good person to work for. Yeah, I will miss Hillhaven.

The party was over at 2:00, and I got my check and other belongings and left by 2:30. I drove past the entrance gate and the guard shack and tears formed in the corners of my eyes. I took a deep breath and said aloud, "This is it, this is really goodbye, almost six years of my life left behind me."

The weather was better today. Again the melting ice and snow made a slushy mess. I stopped by the bank to cash my check and then went to the federal building to pay the IRS two hundred dollars.

Driving home took about fifteen minutes, and when I arrived it was almost 4:00. I suddenly remembered Valerie's party. I had promised her I would be there by 6:30 pm.

I unlocked the apartment door and an odor like cooked food hit me in the face. A smell of bacon and fried eggs. I took a deep breath—now I was sure it was bacon and fried eggs.

I walked carefully to the bedroom. A body was covered up in my bed. I went over and jerked the cover back. It was Mark. He raised up in a sleepy daze and said, "Norma Jean, Girl, I wanted to surprise you, I took a flight here this morning, and I was starving, so I fixed me some breakfast and then I went to sleep."

I reached for him, showered him with hugs and kisses. "Welcome home, Lover," he said, and pulled me under the covers. In no time only soft moans of tender passion could be heard in the room.

Shortly after 5:30 I remembered the party and told Mark we had to go to Valerie's craft show. He frowned slightly and said, "You go on, Norma Jean, you know I don't want to sit around a bunch of women, you know I don't like shit like that."

I said, "Well, we really don't have to stay that long, but I promised Valerie, and she will never forgive me if I don't show."

Mark unhappily consented to go, so we got dressed and arrived at Valerie's around 7:00. The craft show was not a craft show at all. It turned out to be a surprise farewell party for me. A beautifully decorated ice cream cake was on the table, surrounded by other party goodies. Five other people came—Pearline, Donna, Marcia, Helen, and Phyllis. I have known them a long time. We ate and laughed and talked about fun times over the years.

Mark was restless and madder than a wet hen by 10:00 when we bade them good night. They teased us, saying they knew what we were going to do when we got home. Valerie yelled to me from the door. "Norma Jean, I hope you get knocked up!"

I laughed and yelled back. "I hope so!"

At 10:30 we were back at the apartment, and at 10:45 someone called and hung up. At 11:00 Mark still seemed restless and finally said he had to go out for a few minutes but would be back soon. He took off in the mustang, and I heard the car rattling a long way down the street until it became a fading echo.

Mark is so unpredictable, just full of surprises. I wish I could stay awake, but my eyes are closing automatically. I have had a full day today, and my body is giving out. I do wish I could be awake when Mark comes back, but I am not going to make it.

January 16
Saturday, 4:15 A.M.

Fifteen minutes ago while changing positions in my sleep I turned over and felt the soft empty pillow. Consciousness flooded me. Mark had not returned. I got up and fixed a cup of instant coffee. I am really not a coffee drinker. I have always bought it for Mark. He drinks a half cup every morning. I filled my coffee cup, added sugar and cream, and the steaming black coffee turned a muddy brown color.

Where in the hell is Mark? I hope nothing has happened. He didn't even tell me where he was going, but that's typical of Mark. He used to stay out on Friday and Saturday nights, and at first I worried that something had happened to him, until I started finding other women's pictures and love letters he had hidden. Then I knew what was really going on. Mark would always show up early Sunday morning and act as if he was returning home from work. We had a lot of fights about it because he would always lie. Finally I just gave up and stopped being so bothered about it. After all, I have my job and my own friends to fill the gaps of time when he gets restless and high spirited. But I won't have my career and my friends in Houston should he pull this shit and take off in the middle of the night, and then what will I do?

It is now almost sunrise. I suppose I will try to get back to sleep.

January 16
Saturday, 5:00 P.M.

Mark finally came home around 5:30 this morning. I lay quietly in bed, pretending to be asleep. He tested me by sitting on the edge of the bed. I did not move. My head was covered up, and I felt like I was suffocating. After he felt positive I was asleep, he stood and I heard his pants drop to the floor. His metal belt buckle made a clacking sound as it hit the wooden floor.

25

Mark has always slept in his underwear. He has never worn the pajamas I bought him. He pulled the cover over his body, and before I could drift off to sleep, he was snoring loudly in my ear.

I was up by 9:00 but Mark was still asleep. He probably never knew I had gotten out of bed. Before starting breakfast I had this urge to write a poem. My secret ambition has been to publish a book of poetry and maybe write some short stories or a novel. I have been writing poems for ten years, and I have a collection of twenty poems scribbled on pieces of paper. I never even told Mark about my poems. I keep them hidden. Anyway, I wrote this poem around 9:00 this morning:

If Only For One Day

If only for one day, I could be you and you could be me
I would feel what you feel
And see what you see
You would think my thoughts and do as I do

I would walk each mile in your shoes
On your shoulder my burdens you'd carry
I would make my choices by your rules
You would understand and tarry

You would have empathy
I would feel sympathy
We would be like clones, two peas in a pod
And neither one of us could put on a facade

If I walked just a mile in your
Shoes and you carried just half of my blues
I would be eager to give you your dues
And you would know why I break the rules

If only for one day, I could be you and you could be me

I would say kind words to you
And you would say them to me
A happier place this would be
If I could be you and you could be me.
For a day.

I know this poem sounds kind of strange, maybe even schizoid, but it really is symbolic. I mean, if people would stop and think about how their behavior impacts others, it would make a difference. This poem is truly dealing with understanding.

I hid this poem with the others. I have always kept them in a folder stuck in an old suitcase.

I woke Mark at 10:30, and we had breakfast. I never questioned where he had gone. I certainly did not want an argument, definitely not now.

Mark later took the car to the carwash and said he was going to change the oil and do some other things before we get on the road. Everything is all packed, and we will leave early in the morning. I hope the old mustang will make it.

I called Mama and promised to call her as soon as I get settled in Houston.

Everything is done except mailing the change of address card, and I will do that in the morning.

January 24
Sunday, 3:30 P.M.

It has been a week since I have made an entry. I have been busy getting settled. The drive here took about twelve or thirteen hours. It turned my rump into hamburger. I was constipated for three days.

This is a really big city. It gives me a scary feeling like I am going to be swallowed up or something. The interstate system is so different, and it's all confusing as hell to me right now.

Mark took me to the flea market on Saturday. I love flea markets, and this one was the largest I have ever visited. I bought two pieces of depression glass. I started collecting the pink glass two years ago. It was so much fun to look and walk around in the open space.

The weather is nicer here and the temperature was in the sixties today.

Our apartment is nice, a two bedroom with carpet, a dishwasher, and self-defrosting refrigerator. It's pretty bare because our furniture is in storage, but Mark has a king-sized mattress in our bedroom, and the stereo equipment is set up in the living room. The living room and dining room are set up together. In the center of the dining room a chandelier hangs down where the table should be placed.

I have slept late every morning and watched television. I have really needed the rest.

Today I wrote Mama, Valerie, Georgia, and Rachel. I know I really sugar coated everything, but thus far all is fine.

Mark goes to work, comes home in the afternoon, we eat dinner, talk a while, maybe watch a T.V. program, and then he goes to bed. I usually stay up a little later because I don't have anything to do anyway. I feel dependent and have never felt that way before in my adult life. I depend on Mark to take me to the store because I don't know my way around. I went to the laundromat within the apartment complex yesterday.

Maybe next week I will venture out. Maybe I'll put in applications for a job. Social workers are a dime a dozen in this city. I might have to consider doing something different.

I can sense just a tinge of resentment in Mark. He really doesn't like dependency. Even though he hasn't verbalized it, I can feel it. This move is going make or break us.

Chapter Two: February

February 1
Monday, 10:00 P.M.

I awoke today around noon when the sound of someone banging at the door penetrated my deep, almost lifeless sleep. My eyes were swollen and red from crying last night during the "nightmare episode." It is certain that the past, present, and future work together. Nothing about my past can be altered. If a thing happens, it happens. Nothing can change history, yet history makes the present. The past is the reason we are where we are right this minute, and the present dictates the future.

Yesterday began like any other day, a typical day in the life of Norma Jean Williams. Mark went to work a half day, and I stayed in the apartment and slept, read, and then cooked dinner. I have been here for two weeks, and now it is getting harder for me to distinguish one day from the next. I do the same thing every day. Anyway, Mark got home at 2:00, and after dinner he was in a talkative mood. He mentioned to me that I should go to the apartment manager's office on Monday and sign the apartment lease. This didn't make any sense to me because I'm not employed. So I challenged Mark and said, "It doesn't make sense for me to sign it. I don't have a job, and you've already signed, so what's the big deal?"

He looked at me coldly and said, "You are my wife, and you're supposed to sign that lease. I don't want to hear nothing about your not signing it."

That lease was the least of my worries. What I really wanted to discuss was our bills, which we had neglected to discuss during my two week stay. I blurted, "If you want to talk about something, Mark, then let's talk about our bills—like the IRS, the furniture storage fee, furniture bills, the motorcycle note, and things like that."

He was pissed to the highest degree of pisstafication and said, "I am not paying a damn thing but the rent on this apartment, and the rest of this shit can go to hell!" He paused a minute and then continued. "I'm tired of spending my G-D money on unnecessary shit." He was sure angry enough now, and he paced the floor as he vented his true feelings and aggressions. "All this shit to pay, and you quit your job, and you know what? I might be leaving this place. I got another assignment for six months in the Dallas-Fortworth area. So now what're you going to do? You sure can't go with me, and I ain't even found a place to live there, so I guess you're going to have to stay here and find yourself a job. You ain't even tried to find a job since you've been here. Hell, you got a car here, and you act like you're scared or something. You won't even go to the store by yourself. You sit in this damn apartment day in and day out, and two weeks have passed and you ain't done nothing."

Well, that speech brought out years of repressed anger in me, and I said, "Don't you dare open your mouth to say a thing like that! You're the one who encouraged me to come here, and if you had done your taxes right in the first place, we wouldn't be in this mess with the IRS! Hell, I didn't have much of a choice but to come here because the IRS was going to take half my check and I could not run a household off half my salary. And then about working—I have worked throughout our five years of marriage. I have worked,

30

cooked, washed your dirty laundry, and given you sex when you wanted it. I have worked my ass off and for what? For you to stand here and tell me after two weeks of quitting my job that I shouldn't have quit and that I need to find another one? Well, *you* get another one, Mark, 'cause I'm tired, I am very tired of wearing the pants in this family."

It was a very angry and ugly scene, and I stormed out of the room and locked myself in the bathroom. I could hear Mark pacing, cursing, and swearing outside the bathroom door.

The bathroom mirror held my image. My own reflection frightened me as I saw my eyes fill with tears. I looked years older than thirty-one. I really wanted to crack that mirror, destroy it for showing me the truth. The truth is that I am not happy in this marriage and haven't been for a very long time.

I looked at the locked bathroom door and wondered whether I should come out or try living in the bathroom. I really wanted to hide, flush myself down the toilet, or drown in the bathtub.

Then I looked at the medicine cabinet. I opened it and saw two bottles of aspirin with caution caps on the first shelf. Bottles of peroxide and alcohol were on the next shelf. I had a momentary impulse to mix the two and throw the aspirins in as a seasoner. I thought about drinking that stuff, but I knew I couldn't do it. I didn't have the nerve to harm myself like that.

I took a deep breath, unlocked the door, and came out. Mark was in the bedroom, stretched out across the mattress. He turned over as I entered the room. "By the way, a check from your job was in the mail yesterday, and it's on top of the T.V." I walked over, picked up the check, and studied it. I have two more coming, and then my retirement pay will come. After that, I guess I'll file bankruptcy, because my husband has told me he's leaving and I can't go with him. I must either stay in this city and be jobless, return to Knoxville, or go back to my home town. What I really don't understand is why Mark didn't tell me about this move before I quit my job. My alternatives are few, and time is running out. I said aloud, "I guess I'll pay some bills with this money."

He stood up and looked me dead in the face. "Well, I guess the hell you won't—you'd better hold on to that money."

I said, "Mark, the bills still have to be paid, and it sure as hell doesn't help to not pay on them."

He raised his voice. "Why can't you do anything I ask you to do? I asked you not to send in a change of address card, and you did it anyway. I asked you to sign the lease, and you won't do it. Now I just don't know what to say about you."

We were like two live wires. I said, "I think I have complied with your wishes pretty well in almost five years' time. After all, you're the one that leaves and spends entire weekends out. You bring other women's pictures and love letters home! You thought I didn't know that, didn't you?"

He balled up his hands, and his voice trembled. "That's what makes me so mad about you! You gather up bits and pieces of evidence and then use them against me at an opportune time."

I was mad with rage, blinded by anger, and I said, "I am just *tired* of this shit!"

Mark looked at me without blinking an eye. "Well, you know what the hell to do about it, don't you? If you're tired of it, then you can just go to hell whenever you please, take all the damn furniture and the mustang, and do what the fuck you want to do."

An explosion was occurring inside of my body. I grabbed my coat and left. I did not realize my unusual attire until I got in the car. I had on house shoes, a long red night gown, an all-weather coat, and a scarf tied around my head.

The air outside was cold, and it took some time for the car to heat up. After it finally got warm, I drove around for an hour or two. I didn't have a destination, and I really don't know how I found my way back to the apartment. I only know one thing for sure, and that is that I am going to take my black ass back to Knoxville.

When I pulled up in the parking lot, I could see that the lights were out in the apartment and Mark's van was gone. I went in and fumbled for the light switch. When the light flooded the room, I saw an ashtray on the living room floor. Two marijuana roaches were in the ashtray, and the apartment reeked with the smell of weed. He was smoking that shit again. I don't even know how many arguments we have had over the past five years about his marijuana smoking. One time he had a big sack of the shit in our house, and he was talking about how he was going to sell it. I told him over my dead body—no way was I going to live in a dope house. Anyway, it's just been six months ago that he promised me he was going to leave that stuff alone.

I went to the bedroom and started to pack the same things I had just unpacked two weeks ago. I packed a few things, then lay on the mattress to try and get some rest. It was hours before sleep came to me. Rays of light from daybreak were filling the room when I finally drifted off to sleep. Then today this persistent knocking at my door woke me. I fastened my robe over the long red nightgown that I wore last night and then walked to the living room window and peeked out. White powdery snow covered the parking lot, and long diamond-shaped icicles hung from the bottom of the mustang. I peeked through the peep-hole and then opened the door.

It was the postman, and he seemed frustrated at having to stand there knocking in the cold. His nose was rosy and he wore gloves. "I have a certified letter for Mark or Norma Jean Williams."

"I'm Norma Jean Williams," I said, and he indicated where I should sign on the piece of paper. I hurriedly scribbled my name, and he gave me the letter. I closed the door and then looked at the registered letter. It was from the IRS. I did not need to open it, because I knew what was in it. I put it on top of the T.V. in the bedroom. I knew I would not be able to discuss it with Mark. He takes his animosity out on me whenever I mention a bill.

Well, thank God for defense mechanisms. I suppose we'd all be crazy if we didn't have them. I simply chose not to think about the IRS right then. Maybe tomorrow but not now. What I really wanted to do was curl up and hide, but instead I started to clean. There really isn't much to do here, so I made chores for myself. I cleaned the closets.

I went through every pant, coat, and shirt pocket of Mark's, and in one coat pocket I found an airline ticket receipt. It was for the ticket he had used when he came to get me on the fifteenth. I inspected the ticket—the flight number, the gate number, the time and date of departure. Something was wrong. The ticket was dated January 14. That meant that Mark had lied to me. He had been in town for at least twenty-four hours before I saw him.

I got weak in my legs. I feel terribly betrayed; I can't believe anything the man says. Georgia was so right about him. I was disgusted, so I just fell to my knees and lay out on the floor, still looking at that receipt. It wasn't long before the telephone rang, bringing me back to reality. I composed myself and answered, "Hello?"

There was a pause, and then the operator's voice came out clear. "I have a collect call for Mark Williams from Angela King. Will he accept?"

"You must have the wrong number," I said.

The operator questioned the other party and replied, "No, this is the correct number."

I said, "Mark is not here, but this is his wife, and I will not accept the call. Thank you." And then I hung up the phone.

I started feeling a bit paranoid. After the argument, the IRS, the plane ticket, and some strange woman calling Mark collect, I wondered what could happen next.

About two hours passed, and then came another knock on the door. Through the peep-hole I saw that a neatly dressed man and woman stood outside my door. I opened the door, and the man asked, "Is Marcus home?"

"No, he isn't," I replied, and I wondered to myself where he got this "Marcus" shit from.

The woman held a briefcase. She asked, "Do you happen to know when he will be home?" I told her that I didn't.

Then the man said, "We are Stanley and Susan Payne, and we met Marcus a couple of months ago. We're in the soap business. May we come in for a few minutes?" They looked decent enough, so I allowed them to come inside. The man continued. "Thank you for allowing us in your home. You see, we are distributors, and we talked to Marcus a few months back about selling our products on a part-time basis. May I ask your name?"

"I'm Norma Williams, Mark's wife," I answered.

"Marcus's wife?" They said it at the same time, and I repeated that I was Mark's wife and that we have been married for five years. They both looked puzzled. "Please tell Marcus we came by. Here is one of our cards. Maybe we can get together for dinner or a movie or something sometime." I thanked them, and they left.

I collapsed after they had gone, and I slept for a few hours. I have now been writing for an hour. My last thought before I stop is that my entire world is crumbling, and it seems I can do nothing but watch the pieces fall.

February 8
Monday, 11:30 A.M.

I have survived another week of madness. The weather here is now bitter cold, almost as bitter as I feel. It has snowed almost every day this past week, making driving conditions terribly hazardous. There's no way I can return to Knoxville until the weather conditions improve.

Right now I feel like an orphan living in an unwanted home, just existing, not really living.

Mark—excuse me, I mean *Marcus*—came back home last Tuesday evening, and since then we have not spoken ten good words to each other. I did greet him, though. I called him Marcus, and he looked at me strangely. I just don't understand his telling those people his name is Marcus. He lies for no reason—that was simply an unnecessary lie. I have been sleeping on the floor in the other bedroom in order to avoid having any contact with Mark.

I found the IRS statement in the trash. He apparently threw it in there Wednesday morning. I wrote out checks for the bills and mailed them on Saturday. I am expecting another check from Hill-haven in another week. I have six weeks of vacation time built up, and it sure has come in handy.

I still cook dinner every day, but I leave the room when Mark fixes his plate. He sure has a lot of nerve eating my cooking. I mean, I guess it hasn't registered in his brain that I could poison him. I guess he thinks he knows me well enough to believe that I would not have the nerve to do such a thing.

I feel numb, like a frozen vegetable. It's like being dead in a living body. A live dead woman is what I am.

God, help me find some kind of peace within myself.

February 15
Monday, Noon

Yesterday was Valentine's Day, a happy day for lovers. Mark apparently wanted to make up, or he wanted sex, because he brought me a rose in a crystal vase. It might as well have been a weed. Does he honestly think he can say and do the things he has and make it all right by giving me a rose? It probably would have worked a few months ago, but it won't work now.

I was reading in my room on a pallet on the floor when he came in, picked me up, and carried me to the mattress in the other bedroom. He nearly tore my gown off, and then he kissed me passionately. I couldn't feel a thing, and I couldn't fight. I just lay there like a corpse as he had his way with me. My spirit was broken—even murdered—because homicide of the soul is what Mark is guilty of.

When he finished, he went into the living room and played his stereo music and smoked pot. I remained stretched out on the mattress, with his semen dripping between my legs, wishing I could shrink to the size of a paramecium, an amoeba, or any such one-celled animal. This was the worst sex I have ever had. That was my valentine.

36

Now I'm awake, thinking about a funny childhood experience. As a child I was always hiding behind chairs, sofas, or under beds, but the most unusual thing happened once when my mother was going to take a trip to St. Louis because her sister was ill. I remember getting inside the zip-up plaid suitcase, and I don't know just how I did it, but I zipped myself up in that suitcase and then I couldn't get out. When Mama found me, she was amazed. She said, "Lord, child, what on earth made you get in a suitcase? Mama ain't going to leave you." Now those words are so comforting to me: Mama ain't going to leave you.

I am homesick, and just as soon as the weather here is clear, I'm leaving.

February 22
Monday, 1:00 P.M.

Over the past week I have received letters from Mama, Valerie, Georgia, and Rachel. Rachel has decided to start a home for handicapped children. I feel nauseated when I think about having to face them. I can't even bring myself to call Mama—or anybody else, as far as that goes. I feel like a failure, but I guess I knew this was a possibility before I moved here. I mean, we were having problems long before I moved here. But it is a shame I had to quit my job and then move so far away just to find out this shit ain't going to work.

It terrifies me to think I will have to drive the twelve or thirteen hours back alone in the mustang that's not running properly. I believe it has a bad carburetor. Hell, it's probably just old. I keep thinking about the chain saw massacres, and that shit paralyzes me with fear.

Mark, the bastard, has been throwing out hints about his moving to Dallas soon. This man is crazy, and I must have a problem too, since I followed him this far away from home. I set aside my pride and begged him to drive me back to Knoxville. He smiled. "Now why can't you drive yourself back, or get one of your good friends to come down and drive you back? You don't ever consider what I might have to do. Hell, I got to work next Saturday, and you want me to take off from my job to take you back."

I did not say a word, just sat there and silently prayed for strength to do whatever I had to do to get home.

February 28
Sunday, 11:30 P.M.

On Thursday, February 25, I told Mark I was leaving the next day. I put the door key and mailbox key on top of the T.V. and was ready to drive the distance alone. Mark's eyes perked up, and then he softened and said he would drive me.

Wednesday night was another nightmare. Around midnight, Mark heard noises outside. He peeked out front and saw someone tinkering with his motorcycle. He reacted immediately—without thinking or putting on any pants, he grabbed his loaded rifle from the hall closet and went out the front door, aiming the gun at the two white men who were apparently trying to load the bike onto a red truck. Mark stood in his underwear, aimed his gun, and said, "If you move that bike another inch, I will blow your head off. Now put it down this minute."

One of the guys spoke up. "Sir, we were hired by the bank to pick this bike up because you haven't made payments in over three months."

I was standing in the doorway in my gown. Mark yelled to me, "Call the police! I ain't giving up this bike unless the police come."

One of the guys said, "Sir, there's no reason to call the police. We have papers—"

Mark cut him short. "Shut up!"

I called the police, and they arrived in fifteen minutes with the siren and flashing blue lights. The neighbors were now awake, and some were standing outside while others peeked out of their windows. The two white policemen listened to Mark and then to the other guys. Then they reviewed the papers. "Well, Mr. Williams," one said, "it looks like you're going to have to give up your motorcycle. These boys were hired to pick it up. I'm sure if you work out some arrangement with your bank, you can get your bike back." Then the first two men put the bike on the back of the truck and drove off.

I knew then for sure I had to leave soon. I couldn't take much more.

On Friday afternoon we were on the highway heading to Knoxville. The traffic was terribly congested in the inner city. It was sleeting some, but the roads were not too bad.

Mark chose to drive the entire way himself. After two hours of driving, we stopped for food and gas. We gobbled the food down, used the toilet, and were on the highway again.

Anyway, after a hell of a time, when we got near Memphis, Mark started driving fast even though there were sheets of ice on the highway. Alarmed, I said, "Slow down, Mark! Can't you see this freeway has ice on it?"

"That's what's wrong with you," he said. "You're afraid to take chances. I'm not going that fast—couldn't be going over sixty-five."

Our speed on the icy road made me want to vomit. I knew our fate was in his hands. I also knew that the more I talked about the speed, the faster he would go. So I shut up and shut my eyes and tried to sleep.

Then suddenly I was lost in an ancient castle. The huge rooms in the castle were overwhelming. Each room had a tunnel that led to an even bigger room. The rooms kept getting bigger and bigger. The last room had a huge hole in its center. I looked into the hole and saw only darkness. Someone from behind pushed me, and I floated through the darkness until I hit a stream of water. It was clear water, and I could see the rocks at the bottom. Then the sun showed its smile from behind the clouds, and rays of sunlight were everywhere, almost blinding. Then I remembered I could not swim, and my body was slowly going under. A voice from the clouds said, "Hold On!"

Then I jumped at the feel of a hand. My eyes flew open, and I saw Mark wrestling with the steering wheel. The mustang was wobbling back and forth across the road. He said, "Hold on, Norma Jean!" as the car skidded off the road.

The tail of the car switched like a prissy woman, and then I knew we were going to turn over. "Lord, help us," I repeated several times. I closed my eyes and imagined our bodies busted up in tiny fragments and the articles and possessions in the car spreading miles from our bodies. I visualized various sheets of my poetry blowing away in the February winds, lost forever. I could see my Mama crying at my graveside.

The car finally stopped by a rough spot in the ground. It came to a halt like a ball in a catcher's mitt. We were at a standstill; only the sound of the spinning tires eating away at the earth underneath could be heard.

Mark asked, "You alright?"

"I think so," I said, nearly hyperventilating. He opened his door and got out to look at the position of the car. It would require a tow truck to get it out. After about ten minutes of no heat, my hands and feet were getting cold. I could see my own breath as I spoke. After twenty minutes, my hands were feeling numb.

Mark walked to the roadside and attempted to stop several cars. Finally, after what seemed like an eternity, a tow truck came, and Mark flagged him down. In ten minutes we were pulled out of the hole and onto the side of the highway. Mark tested the car before the man in the tow truck left. The car turned over, he paid the man, and we were off again. I was speechless.

Thirty-seven miles from the Knoxville city limit, the car started making a clacking sound. Mark pulled over and looked under the hood and then under the car. Whatever he did cleared up the clacking sound, and we moved on up the road.

We barely made it to Valerie's house. The mustang was on its last leg. When we turned the corner of Walnut Drive and Valerie's house was in plain view right before me, my face lit up.

I have never been so glad to see that house or to be so close to walking up those steps and knocking on the door. It was yesterday—Saturday, at about 4:00 A.M.—when we got to Valerie's. Mark caught a plane back to Houston this morning. It is late, and everyone here is asleep. I guess I should be, too.

Chapter Three: March

March 8
Monday, Midnight

I called Mama last Sunday. I had to call her collect, and I felt bad, but she was relieved. She asked me directly what was wrong. I told her about my returning to Knoxville. She encouraged me to come home, but I knew living in a small town and being black would mean I'd never find a professional job. I do want to go home for a visit, and since it's just about seventy-five miles away, I may go soon.

Mama told me, "Child, I had the worst dream last week 'bout you and Mark. It seemed like y'all was in a car wreck, and the car was all bent up. That dream was so bad I woke up from my sleep, and Child, I bowed on my knees and prayed for y'all. It must have been about two o'clock in the morning, but I prayed 'cause I knew something was wrong." I thought that was strange, because it was about that time that we slid off the road. I did not mention that to Mama.

I have been back over a week, and even though my life is not yet in order, at least I feel a sense of safety here. Hell, safety is important—it ranks pretty high in the hierarchy of needs.

I have received my last work check, and my only other income to expect is my retirement check, which will total about three thousand dollars. I am expecting it in another two weeks or so.

Valerie has been wonderful, assuring me it is okay to stay here as long as I need to, but they don't really have space for me. I am sharing a room with her oldest daughter, Lisa. I thank God for friends like Valerie, and her husband Jack is good as gold.

I am desperate for work. On Tuesday I went to the unemployment office. I was told right off the bat that because I quit my job voluntarily, I did not qualify for benefits. I explained to the interviewer that I quit to move with my spouse. "It doesn't matter," he said. "You quit voluntarily, and therefore you're disqualified for benefits." I wanted to slap his face.

It is strange that a person can work for a lifetime and suddenly find herself in need of help with no place to turn. The man at the unemployment office asked, "Does your husband support you?"

I almost replied, "Does your Mama?"—but common sense took hold instead, and I said, "I just left him, we're separated. I haven't even heard from him in days—now what do you think?"

I just never thought getting some benefits would be so difficult. I mean, I only needed some money to use for job hunting. I have to have gas in my car to get around, and I need personal hygiene items. I know I will find a job doing something, anything. Hell, I could even consider tricking, but I would never get over the guilt.

I envy the people who do what they want to do and don't let anything or anybody bother them. But I should stop these thoughts and use my energies for constructive ventures. I have to move on, but move on to what? I haven't the slightest idea. I keep getting this image of the story that was in the paper yesterday about the man who was lost at sea. Apparently a young man was lost in the middle of the Atlantic Ocean for over a month. He was a good two thousand miles from land and spent all those days and nights alone and just drifting, not knowing what was going to happen. I can identify with that because I feel like I'm just drifting, moving along wherever the stream carries me.

There was a time when I knew where I was going, where I was headed. I wanted simple things—a family, a home, financial security. I wanted to love and be loved. Now I am just grasping at memories and unfulfilled dreams.

My marriage is over. I can never live with Mark Williams again. My money is low, the jobs in my field are few, but I must keep hoping. So I get out every morning and beat the bushes because I have got to find a job, any job.

Tomorrow I go to the board of education, and I'm just praying and keeping my fingers crossed.

March 22
Monday, 10:30 P.M.

Two weeks have passed since my last entry. My world has been rocking! I have some good news this time: I have obtained a substitute teaching job with the board of education. I turned in all the necessary papers today, like a copy of my birth certificate, the results of my TB skin test (I hear TB is coming back again), my college transcripts, and a few other things. The clerk told me that I can start work next week. She has my name on her substitute teacher's roster and will be calling me.

I called the retirement office today and was informed that my retirement check will be here next week. My next venture will be to start looking for an efficiency apartment. The one I moved out of in January is taken. I will start some serious apartment hunting next week.

Mark called for the first time on the fifteenth. He says he will be leaving for Dallas on the twenty-third. I wished him luck rather coldly. He went on to say he had spent a large sum of money on the maintenance of his van, doing repairs that were necessary for his trip to Dallas.

I know Mark so well. What he really wanted to know was whether I had received my retirement check. But I never gave him the slightest hint. When I got on the subject of bills, he was ready to end the conversation. He simply refuses to deal with reality. Our finances are critical, but Mark will not even discuss them.

Last Friday, March nineteenth, I had $10.50 to my name. Bill collectors seemed to come out of the woodwork. The needle on the gas gauge in the car was so close to E they were mating, and I haven't smoked a cigarette in a week. Hell, I can't afford the shit. We take so many things for granted. Sometimes we have so much more than we appreciate or even realize. When I was working at Hillhaven, I used to buy perfumes, colognes, cosmetics, and other luxuries, but now every penny counts. I will be so glad to get some relief and just have enough money to pay my bills and to breathe. You know, if I ever get rich, I'll take one day to shop 'til I drop, and I'll go to Las Vegas and gamble all night. I know I am preoccupied with these things because I am broke.

On Saturday, March 20, I got a certified letter. It was a happy letter, a note from Mama with a hundred dollar money order. I cried as I read her note: "Norma Jean, don't you be trying to tackle all these problems by yourself. Your Mama's going to help you any way I can."

On Sunday, March 21, I called some of my former coworkers. I really hadn't felt up to calling until now. I called Georgia first but never got an answer. I learned later from another coworker that she was in the hospital. I went to see her that same evening. She was on the sixth floor. She was surprised to see me—shocked is probably a better word. Georgia was admitted a week ago because she had some sort of mass show up on an x-ray. She has had several tests done all week long, and thus far no cancer cells have been detected. She was still the same even in a hospital bed. Her first comment was, "You found out that nigger was no good, didn't you?" She continued before I could respond. "I tried to tell you not to move away with Mark. I've always known he wouldn't take care of you. I could tell that by the things he did."

I really didn't want to talk about it, so I quickly changed the subject. "Girl," I said, "aren't you ready to see the sunshine and smell some fresh air after being cooped up here for a week?"

"Girl, I can't wait to get out of here. I'm going to be discharged on Monday."

When Georgia got wound up, she updated me on everybody's personal life. "You know, Girl, Marvin and his wife are getting a divorce. People don't fool me too fast. Rumor has it his wife caught him involved in a ménage à trois with another woman and another man—a threesome!" She was triumphant that her assumptions were right.

All I could think of was Marvin's poor wife. It must have been terrible for her to actually find her husband with other lovers. Their poor little children must be awfully confused. I snapped back when I heard Georgia say, "Norma Jean, since you left there's been a reduction in staff. They're freezing positions as they become vacant. The woman that was supposed to take your position never came on board. They're freezing everything." This was some depressing shit. Georgia is the damn voice of doom, I do believe.

I stayed an hour, but before I left I told Georgia to call me when she got home, or sooner if she needed anything.

As I was leaving, I saw someone at the nurse's station—a tall, dark-skinned man. I thought I had seen this man somewhere before. He recognized me and said, "Mrs. Williams?"

"Yes?" I answered.

"Remember me? I'm David Monroe. I just started to work at Hillhaven when you left."

"Yes, of course, Dr. Monroe, so good to see you again."

"Are you back in town to stay, or are you just visiting?"

"Well, I'm back to stay. I got back about three weeks ago."

"Is that good or bad?" he asked.

What I really wanted to say at this point was, "Would you please excuse me while I have a quiet nervous breakdown?" Instead, I said, "I guess you could say it's good and bad."

"Do you have a job?"

"I'll be doing some substitute teaching with the school system soon."

"Well," he said, "let me give you my number, and give me yours. I'll keep my eyes open for you in case something comes up. You were in social work?"

"Yes," I answered. We exchanged numbers, and off I was in the rattling mustang that Jack, Valerie's husband, had somehow pieced together well enough for me to get around town.

March 31
Wednesday, 11:00 P.M.

On March 26, I started apartment hunting. It's really difficult to find an inexpensive place in Knoxville, especially with the demand for apartments so high right now.

I know I went to at least ten apartment complexes. The most reasonably priced place I could find was a one bedroom on the far southeast section of town. It rents for $190 a month, and water and gas are included. I will have to pay electric expenses. The apartment is located in a rather run-down area. Old houses that haven't been renovated are plentiful in this neighborhood. Loud stereo music came blaring from the upstairs apartment when the manager was showing me the apartment that was soon to become my home.

It has cheap, dark brown carpeting, dingy white walls, and a smell of mildew. There's an avocado-colored stove, a matching refrigerator, and a scarred-up tile floor in the kitchen. The bathroom has a broken light fixture and a cracked sink. This certainly is not the most glamorous place, but it's not the worst I've seen, and the main thing is that it's affordable. I still haven't gotten my retirement check, so I stalled. I told the manager I'd give him a post-dated check, and if he'd get the light fixture repaired, the carpet shampooed, and the walls painted I'd move in when it's finished. The manager agreed and promised to have it done by the first of the week.

On Monday, March 29, my retirement check came. I had three thousand dollars, and the first thing I did was make out a budget.

$700 would go into savings, Valerie would get $150—I will have to make her take it—$380 will go on two months' rent, and the rest will be put on bills to get them caught up to date. I've also got to get some repairs done on the mustang.

On Monday afternoon, I moved into the apartment. Jack got two of his friends, and they moved some of my furniture out of storage. All of it wouldn't fit into my new apartment. I got the necessities, and I'll have to continue to pay storage fees on the rest.

Valerie and Jack are jewels. I will never forget their kindness. Valerie's been especially good to me—she doesn't ask a lot of questions about what happened in Texas.

On March 30, I got my first day of work with the school board. Things are moving fast. I was pushy with the phone company and got my phone service turned on Monday evening. My first assignment will last for two weeks. It's a sixth-grade class at Rose Park School. The teacher sprained her ankle and is under doctor's orders to stay off her feet for two weeks.

I was nervous when I greeted the twenty-two students. The prenatal vitamins and prenatal care must be working, because some of those children are taller and bigger than I am. They might be smarter, too.

I found Mrs. Scott's lesson plans without any difficulty, but I discovered that the children were generally not interested in learning. Some of them talked, others made paper frogs, and some wrote on the board while I was trying to teach class. I was nearly destroyed at 3:00 when the children left for home. I thought long and hard that night about what I could do to make them interested in class. So this morning when they arrived at 8:05, I wrote "my favorite holiday" on the board and instructed each student to write a full page about their favorite holiday. I informed them that I would be the judge, and the winner would get thirty minutes of free time. That caught their attention, and they started writing. For the next task, I had each child stand and tell me his or her goal in life. Some of them wanted to be football players, doctors, nurses, teachers, or singers, but the two oddest goals mentioned came from a girl named Tammy and a girl named Beth. Tammy wanted to be a Bumpmasher, and Beth wanted to be a clown. This brought loud laughter from the other children. I made them listen. "Why do you want to be a clown, Beth?" I asked.

She turned her face, round and plump with big blue eyes, to look at me. "So I can make people laugh. People don't laugh anymore, everybody's always mad, and I want things to be fun. A clown makes people laugh." I thought her reasoning good, so I applauded her. Some of the children clapped also.

I have made it through two days of substitute teaching. I have drawn up lesson plans for Thursday and Friday. Now, I've got to get some sleep—I have a hell of a job to go to in the morning.

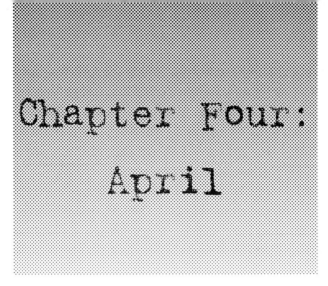

Chapter Four: April

April 2
Friday, 10:00 P.M.

Signs of spring are showing up everywhere. The grass is turning emerald green, flowers are in bloom, dogwood and magnolia trees are budding, and birds are building their nests.

It is not by accident that the seasons exist. Each has its purpose: winter kills off and slows things down; spring brings life and renewal; summer brings warmth and growth; and fall brings ripening and harvest.

Seeing all the Easter colors makes me wonder who started the tale of the Easter Bunny. Why *does* the Bunny carry a basket of eggs? I guess they symbolize life and birth. Anyway, yesterday was April 1, April Fool's Day, and the children were in a playful mood. I talked with them about the seasons. I even tried to get them to appreciate the beauty of nature. I had them write a paper on "The season I like best."

We spent a lot of time talking about current events and people from other countries. Then we talked about desegregation. My class has nearly equal numbers of white and black students, but desegregation is still a touchy subject. They seemed surprised that I introduced such a topic. It's obvious that no one has asked these children much about their opinions on anything. They were all hesitant at first, and then one little black girl named Sherry said, "I think we should have the right to go to whatever school we please."

One little white boy named Corry spoke up next. "I think we should have desegregation," he said. "We don't live in an all white or black world, so we have to learn to get along." I later learned from the school principal that Corry's legal guardians are black. Apparently Corry's mother married a black military service man, and when things did not work out, Corry wanted to stay with his stepfather, who apparently married again and adopted him. He is such a sweet child.

We usually use the first thirty minutes in the morning to either write a paper or discuss a specific topic. So today I talked to the children about doing their best at anything they attempt. Now they know what I expect from them. I decided to test them during the afternoon class period to see if they remembered what we talked about. I instructed them to draw a picture of a house and to put whatever they chose in the drawing.

They got busy. It was quite obvious that some of the children were very dedicated to the drawing while others put forth little effort at all. After collecting the drawings, I showed each one to the class and had them vote on which was the best drawing. Meager, a black boy with unusual artistic ability, had the most votes. He drew a brick house with a balcony, flower pots, and hedges around the house. He drew a tree in the front yard that had an old car tire hanging from one of its branches. Since Meager's peers voted his drawing the best, I awarded him a prize of $1.00. Of course, they didn't know a prize was involved, and one little girl, Sandy, said, "If I had known a prize would be given, I would've done better."

I said, "That's the whole point. Remember this morning, when we talked about doing our best? You must always do your best."

I've had a very busy week, moving and then starting to work. My legs are aching, and my nose is runny. I think I may be catching a virus, or it could be sheer exhaustion. Anyway, I had better get some rest. I cannot afford to take off from work, and I sure as hell can't afford to get sick. I don't have any insurance of any kind—health insurance or life insurance. This is the first time in my adult life I've been without insurance. I feel like I've been reduced to the lowest common denominator.

April 9
Friday, 8:00 P.M.

On the morning of April the third, I woke feeling just awful. My temperature was high, and I ached all over. I tried to eat some canned soup, but it made me nauseous. By noon I felt like I was going to die. I knew I had to find a doctor. It took me an hour to get dressed, and it was an effort just to walk to my car. It was another beautiful spring day; the sun was shining warmly and green grass was budding.

That old mustang smelled of stale cigarettes. Two cigarette butts were in the ashtray, and half a pack of cigarettes rested on the dashboard. The smell made me sick, and the sight of the cigarette pack was repulsive. I threw the pack out the window, dumped the butts out, and drove on. It took me fifteen minutes to get to Dr. Walker's office. He's the only doctor I know of with regular office hours on Saturdays. The fifteen minute drive seemed like an eternity, and I felt as if I would pass out any minute.

I parked the car on a corner lot and then walked along the sidewalk. When I entered the office, the receptionist smiled and then instructed me to write my name on the roster. "Have you been here before?" she asked. I told her yes, two years ago. She asked me to have a seat and said that Dr. Walker would be with me soon.

I sat down and picked up a magazine from a nearby table. All doctors' offices look the same to me, with their tall potted plants, pictures, and magazines racks filled with home decorating and house-keeping magazines.

When the receptionist called my name, I was nearly asleep, the magazine having dropped from my lap.

A nurse greeted me as I entered the examination room. Seeing that I was not feeling well, she rushed through the procedure. First, I had to urinate in a cup, then she weighed me, took my temperature, my blood pressure, and drew some blood. She led me to a private room and told me to take off my clothes and put on the paper gown which was at the foot of the examining table.

I wasn't long—maybe five or ten minutes—and Dr. Walker, a short, slightly overweight, fair-skinned, middle aged man, entered the room. He wore thick, black-rimmed glasses that made his eyes look enlarged. He put his gloves on while he questioned me about my medical status and listened to my description of my symptoms. He listened to my heart and lungs, checked my reflexes, and then called in the nurse as he prepared to do a pelvic exam.

It seemed to have taken forever, but actually he was quite swift. When he finished the exam, he asked me to put on my clothes and meet him in his study. I rushed while putting on my hose and made a run from toe to thigh.

The strangest thought popped into my head. We as a society are so sensitive about nudity and the naked body, yet we undress while our doctors examine us, and the strange thing is we usually don't know our physicians from Adam.

The nurse peeped in just as I finished dressing, and she led me to Dr. Walker's study. He sat behind a large wooden desk. Pictures of his wife and children were scattered around the room, on the walls and on his desk. He was writing prescriptions but looked up and said, "Have a seat, Mrs. Williams." I sat in a brown leather chair across from his desk. He finished writing and then said, "You are pretty sick. Actually, I should put you in the hospital for a couple of days, but I see you have no insurance. Are you able to make other arrangements?"

I shook my head. "No, sir. I really don't have the money to pay for hospital services. You see, I just started to work in the school system, and it's a temporary job, so I don't get insurance benefits."

"What about your husband? Does he have coverage for you?"

"Well, no, he doesn't—but we're separated anyway, and he's in another state." I could feel the veins in my neck throbbing, and my heart was racing. I was nervous—something must be terribly bad for him to want to hospitalize me.

He continued, "You have a high fever, and I've written prescriptions for that. But you must drink lots of liquids and juices, because you've got a bad case of the flu. I've ordered some antibiotics for you, but you need to know that the flu is not the only reason you're feeling unwell. Mrs. Williams, you are pregnant. I'll run the blood work just to be certain, but your pelvic exam revealed sure signs of pregnancy."

"Pregnant!" I repeated the word, and it came at me like a life sentence. He asked when my last period was. Hell, I had not even thought about my period in months because I was so preoccupied with getting back here, getting my own place, and finding a job. But when I thought about it, I suddenly knew I had not had a period in two months. It must have been Valentine's Day. I just sat there wondering what the hell was happening to me and why I have all these problems. The crazy thing is that for almost five years I have actively tried to get pregnant. I wanted it so bad I've even had pseudo-pregnancy symptoms. But now it happens when my life is coming apart at the seams and I'm trying so desperately to get it back together. My wish has now become my curse. So I guess that old saying is true: "Be careful what you ask for because you just might get it."

Dr. Walker stood. "Now you really need to stay off from work a couple of days until your flu symptoms are gone. Call me on Monday about the test results."

I was a destroyed woman when I walked out of his office. I barely remember paying the receptionist or even filling the prescription. My mind was totally preoccupied.

On Saturday I started taking my flu medication, and I woke up early Sunday morning feeling better physically. But I was an emotional wreck. It just keeps bothering me that the worst sex I ever had—I mean, Mark practically raped me—and I end up pregnant. I mean, I just lay there like a corpse, but my egg was apparently in the right place, and now I am left with a baby on the way. But why now? Why did this shit have to happen during this particular point in my life? What should I do? Answers aren't falling from the sky.

I was feeling desperate, and at ten o'clock I went to church to pray for direction. Although the services were comforting, I still didn't have the answers. I did something that I have never done before in my entire life. The choir was singing "I don't feel no ways tired." Well, I was already full of emotion, but when they started on that particular song I heard a loud cry, almost like that of a trapped animal. I looked around, and the ushers were coming toward me with fans and paper napkins. I felt my eyes and my mouth and realized it was me making those sounds. I remember growing up and going to church with my mother when she would sometimes start shouting. Now I know how she must have felt. Anyway, when I got home, I went to bed and just lay there thinking for two hours. I kept thinking, here I am, thirty-one years old, and I am barely meeting my own needs. I thought about Mark; he's almost forty years old, still acting like an irresponsible teenager. I thought about our child. He or she would grow up without a father, because if there's one thing I'm sure of, it's that I am definitely divorcing Mark. Is that fair to this child? If Mark had visitation rights, would he be a good father, a good role model? Would it be fair to the child to bring other men into my life? Hell, I'm still young and will one day want some companionship, if not marriage. How smoothly would that go with a child? If I have this baby, I will forever have ties with Mark. Do I want that? What if I don't have this baby and then find out later I can't have any more children? All these questions have to be answered. I know no one can tell me what to do. I must make my own choice and then be woman enough to live with it.

On Monday, April 5, I went to work. I had to go; I couldn't afford to be off. The only good thing was that the children were now used to me, and I had some control over them. I told them I did not feel well, so we didn't do much talking. I had them write several papers and read.

I called Dr. Walker's office at my noon break and got the verdict. The test was positive. I made an appointment for 4:00 P.M.

Finishing up the afternoon with the children was just horrible. They behaved really well—it was just me going through mental anguish.

At four o'clock I entered Dr. Walker's office and was with him in his office at 4:05. I didn't mince words; I made it plain that I wanted an abortion. He was not surprised, but he felt it necessary to go over the procedure. He said, "I want you to understand the serious implications of an abortion and realize that I cannot be held liable. I have some papers you must sign releasing me of any responsibility should anything happen. There are few complications from an abortion procedure done properly, but there is still some risk. I charge a cash fee of two hundred dollars. I won't accept a check for this procedure. Now, do you need more time to think about it?" I shook my head no. I was glad I had withdrawn $250 from my savings. He got the papers out and called in his nurse to witness as I signed. Then he said, "All right, we can start the process in a few minutes." He stood up and left the room, signaling for me to follow. I followed him to an examination room. He asked me to take off my clothes, put on the paper gown, and then lie down on the table with my feet in the stirrups. The procedure was similar to a pap smear examination, except that he inserted a tampon-like object into my womb. He said, "This has to stay in you overnight. Return to my office the same time tomorrow evening, and I'll complete the procedure. If you have any problems, don't hesitate to call my office or answering service."

After I left the office, I started having some guilty feelings. I wanted to run back inside and ask him to take the thing out, but something pushed me onward. Although I did not have any pain from the insertion, my emotions were drained. I ended up with insomnia, and it was at least three in the morning before I went to sleep.

On Tuesday I went to work. I was exhausted, and the children noticed. Sandy asked, "Don't you feel well, Mrs. Williams?"

At four o'clock I was heading for Dr. Walker's office again. When I got there it was full; at least six or seven women were sitting in the waiting room.

I had to wait for almost an hour, and I was paranoid, imagining the other women could read my thoughts, knew why I was there, and were scorning me. It was simply awful. I know I've had my crazy moments like everyone else, but today I came close to an acute psychotic episode, and I knew it.

When the receptionist finally called my name, I nearly jumped out of my skin. I followed the nurse back to the examination room, and Dr. Walker came in shortly. He asked if I'd had any problems, and after I reassured him, I lay down on the table. He gave me an injection in my thigh, and after about thirty minutes the procedure was complete. Blood dripped from me, and the nurse brought me sanitary napkins. Dr. Walker checked on me and said, "Get some rest. If you have any problems, call me. Otherwise, I should see you in three weeks. Oh, I almost forgot, here's a pack of birth control pills. Start on this pack on Sunday, and here's a prescription for a six-month supply." I thanked him and gave him two crisp one hundred dollar bills.

I was stunned for several hours. I really couldn't believe I had done this shit, but, hell, I didn't have much of a choice. I'm just thankful I could get it done by a professional and that I could make the choice. If I had chosen to have this child, I'd probably have to go on welfare, because I don't even have insurance to pay for prenatal care or delivery. And who would pay my bills during the postpartum period? I sure as hell can't depend on Mark. Anyway, no one will ever know about this incident. If my mother knew, I am sure it would break her heart.

Today is Friday, my last day with my sixth-graders. I will miss them. I also got my first paycheck from the school system today. They mail substitute teachers their checks, and mine was in the mailbox—and very much needed.

I am now near exhaustion and cannot for the life of me say how I made it through this week. God forgive me.

April 16
Friday, 10:00 P.M.

Yesterday was April fifteenth, income tax day, and guess what? I had $800 coming to me, but you know who gets to keep it? That's right—my favorite uncle, Uncle Sam. It's all right with me; I just want to get this account cleared up. Maybe Mark will have some money kept out that will clear up the balance.

I have made it through another week. I was not called to work until Tuesday. I went to Lincoln Elementary School and worked there through today. I was glad I had Monday off. It gave me the time and space I needed to rest and think.

Lincoln Elementary is in my neighborhood, just three blocks away. Today I walked to and from school. It was a beautiful day, and the sun was shining warmly. This afternoon as I walked home in the sunlight, I felt like my spirits were lifting. It was as if the sun's rays were healing me, healing my spirit, healing my soul.

I also noticed something else during my walk. There seem to be an awful lot of young black boys hanging out together on the street corners. It'd be nice if they could get evening jobs or find something more constructive to do with their time.

Getting back to my work day, an interesting thing happened at school today. One of my fifth-grade students told me that she had tried some vodka and had gotten drunk and sick. She went on to say that her mother drinks vodka and smokes pot. I asked her if she had ever smoked pot. She said no but admitted that she smoked cigarettes

59

with her boyfriend. Then I asked her why she drank vodka and smoked cigarettes. "I don't know," she replied.

I said, "Teresa, you are much too pretty to drink vodka and smoke cigarettes. You have beautiful white teeth and a pretty face, and vodka and cigarettes will ruin you." She was amused at this, so then I asked her to write down five good reasons why she should drink and smoke and five good reasons why she should not. After some consideration, she could only think of one reason why she should drink and smoke: because my Mom does it. But she wrote six reasons why she should not: (1) it ruins your teeth and turns them yellow; (2) it makes me ugly-looking; (3) it makes me throw up; (4) it costs too much money; (5) it stinks; and (6) it kills you.

When Teresa turned in her paper, she said, "Mrs. Williams, after I wrote down my reasons, I thought about it. It's really stupid for me to drink and smoke." I felt good that she realized it, but I also felt somewhat like a hypocrite. After all, I just kicked my smoking habit about two weeks ago.

April 18
Sunday, 5:00 P.M.

I am finally getting the apartment in some kind of order. I've managed to hang some pictures on the walls, and I've put most of my books in bookcases, so the place is taking on the appearance of a home.

The walls are thin, and I can hear my neighbors sometimes. My neighbor upstairs is apparently a bachelor and on weekends often invites friends over. Last night he had a party, and I heard people dancing to the music of Marvin Gay, Grand Master Flash, and God only knows who or what else until the early morning hours.

I have been here such a short while, and most days I am at school. I haven't really met my neighbors yet. I know them in passing, but I don't know their names yet.

60

I managed to attend church services today, and I called Georgia when I got home. Georgia is still herself. She's doing fine and is back at work. She asked me about the divorce. I admitted that I've not even gone to a lawyer yet. But I'll make an appointment tomorrow. It's time now.

April 19
Monday, 8:00 P.M.

I have been assigned a five-day sub period at McClain Elementary, and I have a kindergarten class. They have about killed my nerves. I have at least twenty-five students, and the teacher's lesson plan was difficult to follow. Oh, how we forget the little things that mean so much to children at that age! Being first in line carries a lot of importance. So everybody wants to be first. We have to line them up to go to the bathroom, to get water, to go to the cafeteria, and to go outside for recess. My entire work day consisted of lining people up.

The little ones argue over everything. They argue over who gets to be my "helper," and they argue over who sits in what seat. They haven't learned much self control yet, so lots of repetition is needed to control them.

Well, I'm tired and glad I made it through the day. During my break I called a lawyer, a Mr. McIntyre. I saw his ad in the paper—it said "uncontested divorces, $75"—and I scheduled an appointment for Saturday morning. It's kind of strange talking to a lawyer. I have never needed one before.

Anyway, I've been trying to figure out how to reach Mark, because he has to agree to the divorce. Just this evening, around six o'clock, Valerie called. First she told me that Mark had called there looking for me. She wouldn't give him my number and asked him to call back later. I asked her to give it to him because I needed to talk with him about the divorce. The second thing she wanted was to invite me to dinner on Sunday. I could sense that Valerie was up to something, but I had no idea what. I agreed to be there Sunday evening at six o'clock.

April 25
Sunday, 10:00 P.M.

A lot has happened since my last entry. I've completed a week with the kindergartners. On Saturday I went to talk with Mr. McIntyre, and I'll have to go back when I have Mark's address because Mr. McIntyre has to send papers for him to sign. That meeting with Mr. McIntyre was terribly frustrating, but at eleven o'clock Saturday night, Mark called me, and I told him I was filing for a divorce. He said he wouldn't contest it and gave me his address. Our conversation was brief and to the point, and I must say I think Mark was shocked. He probably never thought I would file.

Today I called Mr. McIntyre at his home and gave him Mark's address.

This afternoon I visited Valerie and her family. She had cooked a delicious meal. The aroma of baked chicken, turnip greens, candied yams, and cornbread hit me in the face as I entered the house.

One of her husband's co-workers, a man named Robert Lester, was there. It didn't take long for me to realize that Valerie was playing cupid, but I just wasn't interested.

Robert was tall, dark-skinned, and well-groomed. But he had a strip of gold on a front tooth that glittered when he laughed, and to be honest, that gold turned me off. We are the same age, and he's been divorced for four years. He has two young children and pays child support. He's good-looking, but I don't want any involvement right now. I could tell he wanted to invite me out but wasn't sure if he should move that fast.

I left at eight o'clock, and Robert was still there. Valerie followed me to my car. "Norma Jean, he's a nice man," she said.

I said, "Valerie, he might be a nice man, and I thank you for your trouble, but I'm afraid with the way I feel right now, Mr. Lester would have to have the patience of Job to get along with me. I honestly don't want to be bothered right now."

She shook her head at me. "I wish you weren't so bitter."

"I truly can't help it right now. Thanks for dinner." And I drove off.

Now I'm thinking that maybe I was too harsh with Valerie, but I really don't want to get involved in a relationship right now. It will only mean trouble. After all, what has love ever done for me other than brought tears and heartache? I don't want any part of it.

Chapter Five: May

May 2
Sunday, 9:15 P.M.

I only worked three days last week, and each day I went to a different school. I had the first grade on Tuesday, the fourth grade on Wednesday, and the second grade on Friday. I called the substitute clerk on Monday and Thursday, but she didn't have any openings for me.

Lately I've been thinking that I should put in more applications for work, because school will be out in June and my substituting job will be over. It's frightening to think about, but in June I will be back where I started, looking for work.

Mark called me last night. He said he was sorry for causing me so much pain. I told him I was sorry, too, and as I talked with him, a part of me wanted to be forgiving, wanted to give it one more try. But the long, blood-red gown I had worn the night we had the big argument was slung across my bed. I kept looking at it, and it was that gown, a reminder of the past, that gave me the strength to keep my promise to myself. Deep down I knew that reconciling with

Mark would be my downfall. I am not strong enough emotionally to cope with Mark anymore, and I know it.

I feel kind of sad after talking with Mark, and now I wish I hadn't allowed him to have my number. All those waves of mixed emotions—love, hate, anger—keep creeping back.

I keep thinking that time heals all wounds. Time certainly isn't standing still; it's already May. The year's nearly half over. Yes, time passes, no matter what the circumstances, and people must move on up the street of life.

Now my job, my few friends, and my poems and short stories have become my life. I don't have any interest in dating. As a matter of fact, I shun the single male teachers at the schools where I teach. I don't want to be bothered with the bullshit. They're always giving you some kind of line, and I can see right through them now. Hell, I find my self tensing up or getting angry when a man even makes a pass at me. I suppose I'm just angry about the things that have happened in my life lately.

Maybe I need therapy, or maybe it's just some phase I'm going through. I guess I have some psychological scars. It is a damn good thing you can't see them, because I feel like my very soul has been butchered.

Just now I thought of my unborn child. Perhaps I have prevented a genius from being born. I know I don't need to get on any guilt trip, so let me stop it right now. I just know that I hurt, I ache—not in my flesh, but in my inner self—I'm suffering like hell.

May 7
Friday, 7:45 P.M.

Yesterday I received a beautiful Easter card from my friend from the Czech Republic. Of course, Easter has long since past, but it's the thought that counts. The card cover pictured a beautiful azure sky, grass so green it resembled jade, and a multicolored quilt with patches of orange, yellow, green, and pink spread out near a tree thick with freshly grown leaves. On the quilt was a straw basket filled with different colored eggs. The card read "Happy Easter, please write. Yours, Ava Cheesnova."

I met Ava three years ago when she came to Hillhaven for six months. She was sent to this country via affiliation with the World Health Organization. She is a psychiatrist.

The tall, big-boned, blonde woman looked like an amazon, but she was actually meek and humble. She was also shy. I had known her two weeks before she confided to me that she did not know how to use the water fountain. Some evenings I would give her a ride home to her apartment. She was really a likeable person. She bought a tupperware tea set from me for her daughter. She had laughed— "My daughter shall be the only girl in ma countree wid tubberware." She used to talk about her country a lot. Gas there was two dollars per gallon, and vegetables were brought fresh from the market each day. I can't imagine not eating at least some of my vegetables out of a can.

When she left, she promised to keep in touch, and usually I hear from her twice a year, at Christmas and Easter. I'll write her this weekend. She's sure to be surprised at all the changes in my life.

I needed that card; it certainly lifted my spirits.

May 8
Saturday, 8:30 P.M.

It was a pretty day today, even if it did rain. There was a brief shower this afternoon, and then a rainbow appeared in the sky. It was so beautiful. It's easy to figure out how the story of the pot of gold at the end of the rainbow got started. Something as pretty as a rainbow must have something marvelous at the end of it. I just enjoyed watching the rainbow until one by one the colors faded into one another, then into blueness, and were gone.

I met two of my neighbors today. Larry McCorkle is the man that lives in the top apartment. He's a truck driver, and I'd guess he is in his early forties. He is divorced. I met him at the mailbox, and he introduced himself. I also met Carmen Mason. She lives next to me and has six children. She got a section eight housing grant. She invited me over. I was hesitant at first but went over anyway.

Carmen and I are about the same age. That girl told me her life story. She started to have children at age fifteen. Her oldest daughter, Kim, is fifteen, and her youngest child is five. She bragged about the fact that all of her children have the same father and said their father was married to some other woman and had five or six children by her. She said she got her tubes tied when she had the last baby. Now that the baby is in kindergarten, Carmen enrolled herself in a GED class. When she got her diploma, she decided she wanted to get LPN training, which she is doing now. "One of these days, I am going to get off welfare and take care of myself and my children," she told me. Carmen has never married and said she never intends to marry. Rearing children is hard work, but rearing children alone is even harder. I kept wondering why the hell she had all these kids if she never intended to marry. She's bitter toward men, but she's still seeing the children's father. That doesn't make any sense to me. I encouraged her to continue with her LPN training. I had a hard time believing we were the same age. I mean, six children—that's a hell of a responsibility. A person must be nuts to have that many children to rear alone with no help.

Anyway, it was 6:45 when I left her apartment. I got out my fancy pink stationery and wrote Ava a four-page letter. It's on my dresser waiting to be mailed tomorrow when I go out.

May 9
Sunday, 8:00 A.M.

I awoke early this morning, around 5:30, which is unusual for me on a Sunday. It's Mother's Day, and I called Mama and wished her a good day. I sent her a card with ten dollars. Mama was in good spirits because Janie Mae and her family are visiting. I even got a chance to talk with Janie Mae. She apologized for not calling me, but I know Janie Mae can't afford to call; she has a lot of other responsibilities.

After talking with my family, I could hear footsteps and the shower running upstairs in Larry's apartment. Somehow since I met him yesterday the noise doesn't bother me now. Instead, it makes me feel safe knowing that he's up there stirring around.

Life is interesting on this planet Earth, with its billions of inhabitants, all of various colors, creeds, and religions. We are all the same, yet we are all so very different. Basically we all have the same needs— to satisfy hunger and thirst, to have shelter, to be loved, and so forth—but how we go about fulfilling those needs is what makes us different.

Yes, it's people that make the world go 'round. In the course of a day I may meet or greet many faces, and faces is all they are until I get to know the feelings or emotions behind them. Then, one might ask, what is a person? I suppose a person is really a series of experiences. People carry with them every encounter they have ever had. Our experiences are as real a part of us as the air we breathe.

Well, enough philosophy. Tomorrow I simply must prepare an updated resumé and start scheduling some interviews. In another thirty days, I will be out of a job, and the entire cycle of looking for work starts all over again.

I suppose life would be very dull if we didn't have obstacles here and there. From the looks of my obstacles, I would say I have a pretty colorful life.

May 20
Thursday, 3:26 P.M.

I was not called in to work today, so I called a few places to set up interviews. I have an interview scheduled for tomorrow at 11:00 A.M.

at Oxford Place. It's a residential center for children ages ten through fifteen who have emotional problems. I have a second interview at the Cater Firm for a recruiter's position.

Today a letter came addressed to Mark at the Houston address. The letter had been to Houston and then returned to my address because I'd put in a change of address card.

The envelope was pale lilac with sprinkles of pink and pale blue flowers around the edges. The handwriting was curvy and flowing, very feminine. I opened it and found four pages of love mush poured out and signed by "Jessica." She wrote how she enjoyed their week's stay together when he had visited her in April. She even mentioned certain love-making acts and also said "the other stuff was good, too." That last statement did not make sense to me. Then I grinned, realizing that now I have actual proof of adultery right here before me in black and white.

I really wonder if she knows what she has bargained for. She probably thinks that she has done something smart. She doesn't know yet that Mark has no loyalty to anyone and that she is no more than a pawn in one of his games. Poor little fool.

Kim, Carmen's daughter, came over yesterday. She said they needed some sugar. She said her mother was at the hospital working. Apparently Carmen told her if she needed anything to come to me. I went to my canister and gave her my last cup of sugar. What am I supposed to be, the rock of Gibraltar?

May 22
Saturday, 11:15 A.M.

The interview at Oxford Place on Friday didn't go well. I met with a Dr. Stanton Weir. He's a clinical psychologist, and he's also clinical director of the program. He looked to be around thirty-five years old. His hair was blond, and his skin was creamy white. He had a long, narrow face, sunken eyes, and a long pinocchio nose. His face bore no expression but was very flat, almost lifeless-looking. His shirt was wrinkled, and his too-short pants revealed his white socks. To be a director, he was one of the strangest looking people I had ever seen. He spoke intelligently with a sophisticated voice that didn't go along with his disheveled, unkempt appearance and his blank expression. The man looked stupid as hell.

He described the program to me. The children stayed here anywhere from three months to a year, and most came from broken homes.

I completed the application, and he said he would contact me in two weeks.

I moved on to my second interview with a Mr. Farmer. Four other people were ahead of me to interview for the same job. My interview was brief and ended with Mr. Farmer saying I did not have the experience he was looking for.

I got home around 4:30, and Georgia called me at 5:30. She was on her way over. This would be the first time she had been to my apartment. She showed up thirty minutes later, and she looked to be in good health. Georgia said her doctor told her she was fine and stable. She talked about the old work site and how lots of changes have been made. After an hour of gossip, she got up the nerve to ask, "Norma Jean, how do you bear it? I mean, how do you bear living over here in this neighborhood of bad niggers? Aren't you afraid you'll get ripped off or something?"

"Well, let's see, I think it's called *survival*—that's how I can bear it. Hell, it's the only place I could find that I could afford. Besides, it's really not that bad. You can get ripped off anywhere."

She looked at me for a second and then asked, "But aren't you even afraid? I mean, when I parked outside, I felt paranoid. I kept thinking the minute these people see this Volvo they'll think I got some money or something, and God knows I don't, but so many people are out of work, and I mean over here is the pits. Anyway, I started feeling scared."

I looked at Georgia for a moment and blurted, "Georgia, are you black?"

She looked at me strangely. "Of course I'm black. What are you talking about?"

"Well, if you're black, it only makes sense that you wouldn't be afraid to live with your own kind. I think what's really eating away at you is that you're black but you look white. Maybe you fear you don't belong."

She sneered. "Nonsense, Norma, I just feel that this environment is not conducive to your mental or physical health, and it may not be healthy for your pocketbook, either, if you happen to get mugged. I am talking about your safety."

I didn't want to talk about it anymore. Besides, I have enough fears; I certainly don't need Georgia putting more phobias in my head.

We talked for another hour, and then I walked her to her car. I just wanted to make sure she was safe. She went back to her predominantly white neighborhood and called me when she got home. Georgia has so much book sense but absolutely no common sense. God bless her soul, I suppose she means well.

That was last night, and today I slept until 10:00 A.M. Then I got up and went to the mailbox, where I met Larry McCorkle again. As we talked, I thought he looked burdened, very unlike the other time I'd seen him. Today he looked very old, and like he was losing weight. His waistline was slim, muscles bulged from his shirt sleeves, and his half-opened shirt revealed a hairy chest.

He invited me upstairs to his apartment, and I followed. I felt he wasn't a stranger, because I knew when he got up in the mornings, when he showered or flushed the commode, how many times his phone rang, and when he had parties. He pushed his front door open and I was simply appalled. The living room was immaculate. I felt ashamed of my junked-up apartment.

Larry had two large artificial trees in the corners of the room. A green velvet sofa and loveseat had plush orange and green decorative pillows, and the window sported a hanging orange and green macrame planter with fleshy wandering jew shoots spilling over its sides. A large fan-shaped wicker chair in one corner matched Larry's wicker bookcase. His stereo system rested on a glass and wicker entertainment center. Two nice paintings were hung on the walls, and thick strands of orange and green beads covered the archway leading to the bedroom. "This is a nice place you have here," I said.

"Thanks; it's just some stuff I threw together. Hey, you wanna beer?"

Why not? I thought. In a few seconds, he came from the kitchen with two huge cans of beer—I have never seen cans of beer that large before. He turned on the stereo. Suddenly I sensed something was wrong.

"How is life treating you?" I asked.

He shook his head and replied, "Not too good, 'cause my ex-wife's got a problem. I got three kids by her, and they're almost grown—they're seventeen, fifteen, eleven—and all this time—even when we were together—I worked my ass off trying to give the woman whatever she wanted, and I come home one night to find some other nigga in my bed. Now, I told her then there ain't going to be a marriage no more, and sure enough I moved out the next day. I filed for the divorce, but I ain't had no peace since. That's an evil woman. She wants to take me to court if I miss a week of child support, and she sends the children over here to spy on me like I ain't supposed to have a life of my own. When she gets word that I have a steady girlfriend, she sure enough shows her ass, calling over here, cursing me and my lady friend and raising hell. I'm telling you, if she wasn't my kids' mother, I'd shot the lady a long time ago. That woman is trying to make me miserable. Anyway, about a month ago she got laid off from her factory job, and ever since then all I hear about is money, money, money. Even though I send my child support payments through the court, she's still wanting me to give her more money, and she had the nerve to tell me she's thinking about going back to court to get the sum of child support raised. I told her it'll be a winter storm in hell before I give her another damn cent above what she's getting, 'cause she buys her niggas suits and shit. Then I just told her I'll take my damn kids and raise them myself, and she said she'll be dammed if that's so, and finally I just hung up talking to her. About two hours later one of her brothers called, and he tried to get smart, and I told him to mind his own damn business. She's got six brothers and always has them in her affairs, and they're a hellish kind of people; they like to keep a mess going. So I'm sitting here thinking maybe the best thing for me to do is to just move out of town, maybe even out of the state, 'cause if I stay here, it's going to be trouble, 'cause I keep my pistol with me all the time." And he pulled a pearl-handled gun from his trousers, and I felt nervous until he put it back. "Yeah, I think what I'm going to do is leave after my next trip. I got a run to St. Louis tomorrow and oughta be back on Tuesday. I guess I'll just hat up then."

I sat quietly and listened. I actually felt sorry for him. I didn't think I could feel sorry for any man, but I really did. After finishing the beer, I told Larry that I hoped things would work out and that I would say a prayer for him. I walked down the steps leading to my apartment, saying a silent prayer for Larry. I could thank God that I didn't have his problem and that no children were involved in my situation.

May 28
Friday, 11:00 P.M.

My substitute teaching days are practically over. June 4 will be my last day. Thank God I worked all this week. The kids are getting exceptionally restless. They're tired and ready for summer vacation.

I taught fifth grade at Bob Joy school all this week. Yesterday one of the boys in the class dropped a note he had written to the girl sitting in front of him. He was unaware that he had lost the note. I picked it up later after the children had gone and read it.

From: David R

To: Brandi B

Will you go with me for the rest of the year?

Yes   Hell No   Maybe

()   (X)   ()

P.S. Sorry for the put down but you are a BITCH

Someone had put an X in the the "Hell No" slot. I felt they needed a lesson on social skills, so today we talked about showing respect to one another. We also talked about what it means to be a bitch. Surprisingly, none of the children commented, so I had to call the young boy, David R., who had written the note, to explain it to the class. Well, he couldn't, so I got a dictionary and had Mr. David R. stand before the class and read the definition. Initially he spoke in a low voice, but I told him to speak loudly. He read, "Bitch...a female dog or other canine animal." I asked the class if they knew the meaning of canine, and nobody spoke up. So I found "canine" in the dictionary and had him read it. "Canine...of, pertaining to, or characteristic of a member of the family Candidae, which includes dogs, wolves, and foxes." I told David to be seated and further explained that the author of the note I found with "bitch" on it was mistaken, because to my knowledge, there were no female dogs, wolves, or foxes in the classroom. We went from that to a discussion about dating and what is expected of males and females in the dating game. Then we played the Dating Game.

Now, on a different note, I think I may have a lead about a job, but it may mean relocating. Anyway, the interviewer will be on the university campus about two weeks from now.

I called my attorney, Mr. McIntyre, on Monday afternoon to inquire how things are progressing. He told me that he mailed the papers to Mark and that he is awaiting a reply.

It seems this business of getting a divorce is not always simple and sometimes takes a while. One thing in my favor is that there are no properties to split and there are no children to argue over.

But still, getting a divorce is a lot more complicated than getting married.

This reminds me of Larry. He went on his trip to St. Louis and returned on Tuesday evening. I know because I heard him upstairs moving around.

On Wednesday evening near seven o'clock, Larry knocked on my door. I let him in and invited him to sit a spell. He seemed awfully troubled and said his ex-wife had made all kinds of threats against him. He had warned his girlfriend not to come by. He also said he couldn't leave town just yet, because he still has two more runs before his company will transfer him.

Larry had been drinking beer, and lots of it, because I could smell it from a distance. I could see the outline of the pearl-handled gun in his pocket. He says he carries it everywhere. "My Little Buddy," he called the gun, and he patted his hip. He assured me I had nothing to worry about. "If you have any trouble, hit the ceiling. If I don't get them coming in, I'll get them coming out."

Somehow I felt safe with Larry upstairs. I hardly knew this man, but I was sure I had nothing to fear. He's just so sad, his face showed such grief.

I suggested that he get legal counsel and go to the police if he got any more threats from her or her family. He nodded, but I knew he would not take my advice.

He trusted me. It's strange, but sometimes we share our innermost secrets with people we barely know. "Listen here," said Larry. "I ain't never told nobody this, but I got a deposit box key planted at the bottom of my flower pot. You know, the tall plant in the living room. The key goes to First National Bank. I've got some important papers and things in that box. I've also got about $500 cash money in an envelope under the carpet in my bedroom. I ain't never told nobody this, but if something happens to me, I want you to call my mother, Mrs. Daisy McCorkle. She lives in Little Rock, Arkansas, and—here—I'll write the number for you." I gave him my address book, and he scribbled down the name and number. He continued,

"If you can't find me or something, call her and tell her to come and get the deposit key and the money. Will you do that for me, Norma?" I said yes. He said he had another run on Thursday to Chicago and would be back on Friday night. I wished him luck and said a silent prayer for him as he left.

I don't know if Larry is back. It's now almost 11:45, and I haven't heard anyone stirring around upstairs. If I don't hear any noises tomorrow, I'll go investigate.

May 29
Saturday, 6:00 P.M.

I feel just awful. I haven't heard any noises upstairs all day, and now I'm really worried. I don't know if I should call the police or not, and if I do, what am I going to say?

This is awful. I even went and knocked on his door this evening. No answer. This whole thing makes me feel so damn eerie.

I don't know his girlfriend's name or number, so I can't even contact her. I debated for over an hour whether or not I should call his ex-wife and finally decided I would. So I looked her up in the phone book, and there is only one Lucille McCorkle on Tucker Lane. She sounded like she had been napping, and she really didn't appreciate me calling about Larry. She said she had not seen him and didn't give a damn if she ever saw him again as long as he paid his child support money. The burning hatred in that woman's voice could probably melt steel. I don't want to call his mother yet, because I don't want to alarm her for no reason.

I swear I've never felt so frustrated and helpless in my life. I just don't know what to do.

May 30
Monday, 1:00 A.M.

I cannot believe what happened today. I feel saddened and puzzled. At two o'clock this afternoon I couldn't take it anymore, so I contacted Larry's mother, Daisy McCorkle. She hadn't heard anything from Larry in weeks. "I tell you," she said, "I worry about Larry, 'cause he's had some problems with his ex-wife. That woman must be a witch— did he tell you she had her no-good brothers break into his place and steal a lot of his things about a year ago?"

I said, "No, ma'am, I didn't know that."

She paused for a minute and then said, "I'm going to catch the first bus going that way."

After we hung up, I took a bold step, fearing what I would find. I called the manager's answering service to get him to come over and open Larry's door. Then I called the police.

The manager was fussy about having to come out on Sunday to open a door for what he thought was nonsense. We waited for the police, and they arrived in about ten minutes. The manager seemed nervous. I wanted to run when the key clicked in the door and revealed the immaculate living room. It was quiet inside. The policeman went in first. He pulled the orange beads aside and stepped into the bedroom. The manager and I followed nervously. We entered the bedroom, and there he was. He was leaned back in a chair, his body frozen, his eyes staring into the ceiling. I screamed, "Oh, My God!" His half-packed bag was at the foot of the bed, and it looked as though he'd started packing and decided to rest for a moment. I started to scream again, and the policeman escorted me out of the room. He called an ambulance and asked if I knew Larry's next of kin. I told him his mother was on her way, and I went hysterical again. When the ambulance arrived, the officer suggested they give me something to calm my nerves. The attendant told me to go to my apartment. Did I have some muscle relaxers? Yes, I did. I took two, and it wasn't long before I was asleep.

I finally awoke at midnight, and the realities of the day slowly crept back into my consciousness. The telephone rang, and it was Larry's mother. I invited her to come down to my apartment, and she did. Larry didn't look anything like his mother. She was puffy in the face, and her eyes were red from crying. "You know, they're saying that Larry had a heart attack. I never knew him to have heart problems, but the police said it looked like he'd been drinking heavily, and they found some cocaine. They believe the combination of the two drugs may have caused him to have a heart attack." I didn't know Larry used drugs. I asked his mother if he had a history of drug abuse. She said, "Larry had a little problem with drugs a few years ago, but he got some help and seemed to be doing all right. I hadn't heard about him using anything in over five years. But I guess the pressure his ex-wife has been putting on him would probably drive a saint to the same thing."

Mrs. McCorkle got the money and the safety deposit box key, but she said there was no gun. The police didn't find a gun either. That was my clue that something was wrong with this picture, because Larry kept that gun on him.

I didn't tell his mother. I won't tell anybody, but I believe someone was there with him when he died.

Perhaps a heart attack, a stroke, drugs, or something else killed Larry. Whatever happened, I think more than anything else, just trying to live is what killed him. It seemed the more he tried to carve out a life for himself, the more obstacles got in his way. I guess sometimes people get tired, and they give up.

Chapter Six:
June

June 4
Friday, 8:30 P.M.

Today marks the closing of school for summer vacation. I don't have
a job yet, or much energy to look for one.

I haven't gotten over Larry's death, and I feel uneasy. It's not like I
knew him for a long time, but he talked out his worries and fears
with me, and I got to know him. Now it seems he's gone as quickly
as he came into my life.

Sometimes I wonder if foul play was in the picture. I mean, his
gun wasn't on him and was never found. But I don't know how anyone could have gotten into his apartment forcefully without Larry
shooting them. There are just too many pieces to this puzzle, and it
makes my head ache to try and figure it out. I only know something
is not right. It just doesn't feel right.

The funeral was in his hometown. I couldn't go, but I sent some
flowers and asked his mother to keep in touch.

The apartment above me is now empty. I don't hear any stirring
to indicate life. I do miss Larry, God bless his soul. I hope I find the

pieces to the puzzle of his death. But if I don't, I hope I can find the strength to deal with it.

Well, for some reason I cannot worry about a job now, although I need one. I suppose sometimes in our lives we encounter things bigger than ourselves, things that make us forget ourselves and our own little problems and let us know that we are compassionate.

June 12
Saturday, 11:30 P.M.

On Saturday, June 5, I packed a bag on impulse and drove to Crossroads. I didn't even telephone Mama that I was coming.

The drive did me good. I thought aloud, reminisced and sang songs with the radio. The scenery was beautiful. Plentiful green leaves hung from thick trees, flowers of every shade peeked at me along the roadside, and in spots honeysuckle was blooming. The sky was deep blue with sprinkles of translucent white clouds that looked as though someone had taken an armful of white mist and thrown it into space. The sun was a round ball of glowing gold, casting a tint of amber on the trees, flowers, and the highway I traveled.

I had a desire to paint this pretty picture or capture the very instant of the beauty that surrounded me. But I can't paint, so I held that image in my mind until now when I can write out the feelings I had when I approached our house. "Home." I felt secure and thought that it's so good to have one to go to.

My mother's flowers were plentiful around the white frame house with the well-kept yard. Mama has always loved working in her yard. I drove the mustang up the driveway and gave a sigh of relief as I clicked off the ignition. I took a deep breath and got out of the car. The air smelled fresh, clean, and warm.

The door was locked, so I reached my hand into the mailbox to find the door key tied to a shoestring. Mama always leaves the key in the mailbox when she goes out for the day. She always says, "Never know when my children may take a notion to come home, and I want to be sure you all can get in."

In a town like Crossroads, everybody knows everybody, and I felt myself really missing that protectiveness and the safe, secure feeling you get from small communities. That's the kind of community I grew up in, right here in Crossroads.

Some folks say you don't have any freedom when you live in a small town. Some years ago, I would have agreed. It seemed that if you ate soup for breakfast, the entire town knew it. But that's not so bad, especially when you're free to leave a key in a mailbox or sleep on your front porch without any worries. I'd say that's the best kind of freedom.

I unlocked the door and went inside the old, familiar place. My first stop was the kitchen. I opened the refrigerator and got out the pitcher of grape Kool-Aid. I poured myself a big glass. As I sat at the kitchen table, I sipped the drink and thought of my father. He used to call Kool-Aid "penny drink," because they used to buy it for a penny. Well, that certainly is not the case now. I finally finished the last drop and made myself get up and walk down the hall to my old bedroom.

Mama had taken the old twin-bed furniture out, and now a full-size bed and accessories were there instead. I sat on the bed and bounced. It was nice and firm, but I wanted my old bed back. Mama had moved it into the next bedroom—I could see it from the doorway.

I went into that room and stretched out on my bed. In ten minutes I was asleep. I woke an hour later to Mama's voice. "Child, your mama is glad to see you! Eddie Sue 'cross the street called me over at my housecleaning job and said 'Gal, I believe one of your children is home, 'cause there's a car in your driveway!'"

I raised up, blinking my eyes and trying to get the sleep out of them, and I reached for Mama and hugged her. She sat down at the foot of the bed, and we talked for an hour. Then she said, "Just lay on down, Child, I'm going to fix us some dinner, and I'll call you when it's ready."

Well, me and Mama ate a big supper, and I washed the dishes while she sat at the kitchen table talking to me. We talked about Crossroads and all the changes it's seen. A new mayor, some apartments being built across the railroad track, and so on. Then we talked about Mark, and I confessed that I still cared for him, but I knew I could never live with him again. Mama was a comfort to me.

Anyway, I stayed in Crossroads until today. It was painful for me to return to the realities of my crumbled-up life and this fearful, paranoid city.

June 13
Sunday, 10:55 A.M.

My body feels better, and my nerves are calmer. Going home did me a world of good.

On Tuesday I have an appointment with Mr. Ralph Washington, a recruiter from D.C. He will be at the university. So I'll rest tomorrow. I am really glad I paid two months' rent when I moved in this place, because it may be a while before I get a job.

Anyway, I think I'll call Valerie and maybe Georgia after church. I feel like I need to socialize some.

June 13
Sunday afternoon

I visited with Valerie, and things aren't good. Jack has gotten laid off from his job. Valerie was appalled at the fact that unemployment can peak at $110 a week. "Nobody can live off that!" she said, and I agreed, but then later I thought that I'm not even getting that. I didn't qualify for benefits or food stamps, so I guess you might say I lied, because I am definitely living off less than $110 per week.

I left Valerie's and returned home. I called Georgia, and she sounded cheery. We talked for an hour, and she carried on about how I needed to move out of this section of town. I kept thinking to myself that it's easier said than done. I don't even have a job. I know I can't move, and after talking with Georgia I felt depressed.

June 19
Saturday, 4:50 P.M.

My week has certainly been different. On Monday, June 14, I contacted my lawyer, Mr. McIntyre, and he said he hasn't received a reply from Mark. I know Mark has the papers. He's just acting contrary by not signing them. Anyway, nothing has been settled yet about the divorce.

On Tuesday, June 15, I took my time in dressing for my interview with the man from D.C. I wore my black suit with the skirt that has a slit on the side and the matching jacket. I wore gold accessories and black bare-backed high-heeled shoes.

When I finished dressing, I checked my appearance in the mirror, and my reflection looked like a new person. I realized that I've simply been neglecting myself for the past six months. I haven't been wearing make-up or even trying to look appealing.

My nails were manicured and polished with a mahogany hue that matched my lips. My curly hair picked out just right, and my body had the fragrance of a sweet perfume.

I must say I was decked out in black—it's a witch's color, and I did feel wicked.

I met with Mr. Washington at 2:30. He's a short, slim man with pecan-brown skin and specks of freckles on his face. His hair was neatly cut and revealed a receding hairline. He had small, slanted eyes and a mustache. He was attractive—mature, yet somehow boyish at the same time.

He described the position to me and stated that if I got the job, I would of course have to relocate to the Washington, D.C. area. I gave him a resumé, and he reviewed it carefully, then gave me an application to complete.

The interview was over in forty-five minutes, but I could tell Mr. Washington was stalling. He finally invited me to have dinner with him that evening and gave me the number of his hotel room. So at 7:30 I called Mr. Washington, and he sent a taxi for me. He met me in the hotel lounge, and we had drinks.

I must have had at least three Bloody Marys before we ate dinner. After the meal, we returned to the lounge where a band was playing and people were dancing. I felt wild and free, and I ordered more Bloody Marys. We danced and talked and laughed.

Washington has travelled extensively. He's visited Europe several times and been to forty states. We talked about languages, and he said it's really strange how words mean one thing in one language and mean something completely different in another. For instance, "a big wheel" translated in French means "a big cabbage." I laughed for fifteen minutes. I have never been so drunk in my life, and when the lounge was closing, he almost carried me to his room. When he gestured to me and finally undressed me, I did not resist. Hell, the feel of someone's flesh next to mine was an overwhelming sensation. It had been so long, too long, and I couldn't fight it.

He was a slow, dedicated lover, teasing my nipples and my earlobes until I nearly burst with pleasure. But even though I needed this, I could not reach an orgasm. That didn't stop him, though, and he held me softly afterwards, with his arms and his body half covering mine like a protective shield. I went to sleep and woke the next morning in the arms of a man I didn't even know. My first reaction was to jump up and run because I had obviously gone crazy in the head. But Washington said, "You have made me so happy, my dear. I will never forget it. We must eat breakfast," he said in a fatherly fashion, and he ordered room service. I looked closely at him. He was at least fifteen to twenty years older than me. I wanted to know everything about him, but then again, I wanted to know nothing. I did get the nerve to ask of his family. He was divorced, he said, with two sons—one in college and the other about to graduate from high school.

After breakfast I said I had to go. He assured me that I had the job and made me promise to call him or come by again that evening. He said he would be leaving on Thursday morning. I gave him my number, and he gave me his office number in D.C.

I left the hotel at 8:30 after having spent the night with a stranger. Five years ago I would've never done that. I am learning new things about myself all the time. The divorce process and my life's crisis has turned me into a person I don't even know.

I was home by 9:00 with nothing to do, and I wondered why I had even rushed back to this quiet, lonely place.

I wondered if anyone had called me. By 11:00 I was sleeping and had already planned to meet Washington by eight that evening.

At 3:00 I got a call from Georgia. She sounded extremely disturbed. I kept asking her to tell me what was wrong. "I called you so many times last night, but you weren't home. I was calling to tell you about this awful thing that happened to me. Please come over, and let's talk." I left immediately for her house and I was there in twenty minutes. Georgia's face was bruised, and she looked like a scared animal. I didn't know what had happened, but I felt sorry for her and gave her a hug. Georgia said, "Girl, you ain't going to believe this shit, but late yesterday evening, almost dark, I was doing some light grocery shopping at the supermarket on the corner here where I live. There were only a few people shopping. Anyway, I think I may have had ten items, because I got in the express lane. There was a young white man in front of me. Well, he was talking with the cashier and the next thing I knew, he pulled out a sawed-off shotgun and told the clerk if she cooperated, no one would get hurt. He instructed me to hit the floor and not look up. I did exactly what he asked me to do. The cashier emptied her register and gave him the money. There was another guy at the entrance of the store—his accomplice. The guy told me to get up and get my car keys out. I did, and the two of them followed me to my car. They put on their masks and said we were going for a little ride. I tried to talk with them, but the mean one told me to shut up. Then I was out on a dark road and that mean one smacked me around and told me I'd better never tell anybody about this. They left me out there on that dark road. A man driving an eighteen-wheeler stopped and picked me up. This shit was like something out of the movies. I'm afraid that they'll find me. After all, they still have my car, my purse, and all my identification papers." I couldn't let Georgia stay alone, so I made the decision right then to spend the night. I called Washington and canceled our date.

On Thursday morning, Washington left for D.C. I phoned him before he left.

Georgia didn't rest well at all. I finally told her she had to get some therapy, and I called and made an appointment. I also told her she had to report this to the police. She was too afraid, so I called and gave the information. I phoned Georgia's sister, and in a couple of hours she was there.

I was back home at 8:00 Thursday night, and Friday I slept, and today I slept, and during my two-day absence, someone has rented the upstairs apartment. I heard the noises of people walking, and then I heard a masculine voice.

I thought of Larry, Georgia, and myself, and it seems as though the world is going mad. Is this shit for real? Is someone playing a joke? Has everybody gone crazy? Too much is happening too fast, and I don't understand it. It's getting to the point that I am afraid to wake up in the morning, afraid I might be confronted with some shit I can't handle.

June 28
Monday, Noon

I was just thinking about how some people's futures are already provided for, because they seem to have everything they need and want. For instance, if a wealthy couple has a baby, I'm sure there's a big celebration, and the child will grow up feeling very special. But what about the child that hasn't been planned? What about when there's barely enough money to buy formula and diapers? Is this child going to feel special? I doubt it. Anyway, let me get back to my world of looking for work.

Last Wednesday, June 23, I went on an interview with the Employment Security Office, and I got a job! I'm to start work on July 1 as an interviewer, and my salary is not too bad.

On June 24, Washington called and said I had the job and should relocate in three weeks. Initially I was excited, until I asked for his home number. He paused a moment and then said he couldn't give it to me because his long-lost divorced wife had suddenly come back after seven years of separation. I told him to please add "and they lived happily ever after," because that was a fairy tale if I ever heard one. Finally, I just told him to keep the job and go to hell. I slammed the receiver down angrily. That bastard was married all along and told me that damn lie. Hell, he didn't have to lie. As hard up as I was, I would probably have gone to bed with him anyway. I am beginning to feel like I can't trust a word a man says. I mean, are all men sociopaths? Better yet, am I attracting sociopaths? Anyway, I could kill him for lying to me. He must have called right back, because the telephone rang, but I didn't answer it. It took me two days to get over my anger.

On Sunday, June 27, Mark called, and this time he sounded angry. He announced that he was not going to consent to the divorce, and then he accused me of wanting to be with someone else. I listened to about as much of that bull as I could stand, and then I hung up.

Now it's Monday, and I have had it. I'm looking forward to starting work on Thursday. Anything to stay busy and keep my mind occupied before I fly the coop.

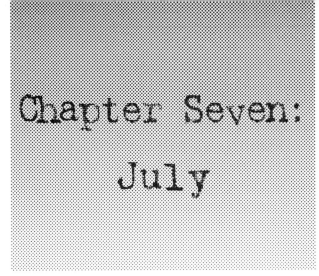

Chapter Seven:
July

July 6
Tuesday, 6:00 P.M.

The weather is giving us pure summer heat, and the air conditioner in this apartment is no better than a high-speed fan. I am perspiring as I write this.

I have so much to write, I really don't know where to begin. I guess I'll start with my first day on my new job.

The employment office is located downtown. Parking fees are simply unreal downtown, so I rode the MTA bus. I was up at 5:30, dressed by 6:30, and on the bus at 7:15. At approximately 7:50, I walked into the security building. A dishwater-blonde woman was seated behind the desk, and she gave me a W-4 form to complete. At 8:15 she led me to the elevator and went with me to the twelfth floor. I followed her to the end of the hall, into room number 215. She pushed the door open and revealed a small, closet-like room with a table, six chairs, and several big boxes. The table had one glass ashtray and a stack of sticker labels on it. "Mrs. Herron will be here soon to explain what your task is for the day." She left abruptly. Ten minutes later, another tall blonde woman came in. She wore a rainbow colored dress and ice-blue shoes. Her hair was shoulder-length and curly. She had blue eyes, a heart-shaped face, and a long thin nose that peeked out over red-painted lips. She had a deep southern accent. "I'm Phyllis Herron. You must be Norma Jean." We went through the introduction process, and then she told me that other people would be joining us. Then she explained what our task would be. We were to put address labels on envelopes and mail letters to all the businesses in the state. These letters contained information about increased employment tax. Phyllis took a battery-operated radio from her purse and set it on the table. "You have to have something to keep you going on this job," she said.

We started with the labels, and fifteen minutes later, Jane, a dark-haired white woman with tanned skin, walked in. Jane and Phyllis are close in age—I think they're about fifty years old. One by one the workers came in: Thomas, a guy with papersack-brown skin came in, then Jimmy—a white guy with a mustache and cowboy boots. David, another newcomer, came in next. He had baked-brown skin with marbled brown eyes. He was shy. Phyllis introduced everybody. We all had our space at the table, and we were working steadily with the labels while country music played from the radio and filled the room. Phyllis is friendly and a big talker, which helped pass the time.

On my first day at work, I stuck about 2,800 labels on envelopes, and the group covered thirty different conversation topics on everything from marriage to shacking up. I think I listened to about a hundred country music songs. I can truthfully say I now know something about country music. I mean, I kept hearing the names of the Oak Ridge Boys, Alabama, Patsy Cline, and Loretta Lynn over and over.

When I got home, I could think of nothing but labels. My hands had developed an automatic rhythm, and I knew the lyrics to "Coal Miner's Daughter." Well, it's a job. It's not hard work, not very creative—a conditioned monkey could probably do it easily—but at least it's keeping some food on the table and a roof over my head.

The second day, Friday, July 2, was the same thing. Jane predicted it would probably be mid-week before we finished the labels. Then I asked what we would do then. Jane just smiled and said, "Well, we'll be given new assignments."

On Friday, Thomas talked about one of his former wives. He's been married three times. His third wife was ten years older than he, and she stripped him of everything when he filed for divorce. I didn't speak of my situation. I just can't talk about it yet. You know, it seems no one likes the people they married. I can count on one hand the people I know who are married and really seem to like each other. It seems that married people go out of their way to upset each other.

I left work at 4:30 and caught my bus at 4:40. I do like the idea of leaving work at the same time each day. I was home by 5:05, trying to plan something to do for the weekend. Monday, July 5, was our scheduled holiday, because the Fourth fell on Sunday.

I called Georgia, but she was out with her sister. Her mother answered the phone. "They're gone to the mall," she said. "Just left a few minutes ago."

I thanked her, hung up, and went to bed. I must have been more exhausted than I thought, because I fell asleep in my clothes on top of my bed, and I slept until 8:30 the next morning.

On Saturday morning, at ten or eleven, the phone rang. It was Mark, and he was in town and wanted to come by. I told him out front that he was not invited. Besides, he didn't know where I lived. At this, he said he did know where I was, and he gave me my apartment number. "How do you know that?" I asked.

"'Cause I've had a private detective following you, my dear, and I know every step you've made since May. Yes, every step, and I'll tell you something else—I got the damn divorce papers, and I'll be an idiot in the third degree before I sign them. I am not signing them damn papers, ever."

I was shakened. "I don't see why not," I said. "Mark, you have never wanted a wife. Why the hell don't you admit it? All I ever was to you was some kind of glorified girlfriend. You never treated me like a wife, always going off for two and three days at a time and me not knowing your whereabouts. Not to mention your girlfriend calling me! Hell, need I go on?"

There was deadly silence for a moment, then he said, "I don't care what you say, you're my wife, and I'm not going to sign any papers!"

I gathered my strength. "Mark, it's true I loved you, and I still care despite everything. I still care about you, but I will never live with you again. I simply cannot cope with being married to you. You take me for granted, you take my love for granted. Mark, love is a very precious, priceless gift. One human being caring for another is so special and so significant that when love is taken for granted, it is smothered. It's like a burning flame. If you feed the fire, it continues to burn, but if you ignore it, it goes out. What was once burning between us has become a smoldering piece of ash. So, Mark, you may not cooperate by signing the papers, but that really doesn't stop anything because the damage has already been done. Contesting the divorce does not make us a married couple anymore than the signing of the marriage license. Those things are only symbols, Mark. True marriage commitments are made in the hearts and minds of people. Now, why don't you just get out of my life?" Mark didn't reply. He just hung up the phone. I held the receiver for a few seconds and then dropped it. I felt saddened, weak, and nauseated, and I cried. I cried softly and then aloud and finally took a cloth to wipe my eyes. Then I went back to bed to the safe escape of sleep.

On Monday, July 5, I awoke early with a stuffy feeling. My body craved fresh air, so I dressed in short pants, a short-sleeved top, and tennis shoes, and went for a walk to rid my body of some stress.

The sun was shining brightly, and the hot air felt like heat from an oven. It was scorching hot. The air smelled of charcoal, smoked meat, and barbeque sauce. The street was busy with traffic. People were going to the park to Fourth of July reunions, to the fair, and God only knows where, but people were going places, and I was walking in the hot sun. Beads of sweat lined up on my nose and neck and streamed from my forehead, but I kept walking like a driven maniac. I had this compulsion to walk until I fell. I must have gone three miles before I stopped. I had made it to the park. There were crowds of people everywhere, and at every park bench and table, there were baskets of food, grills with food, and coolers with iced sodas, beer, and other drinks. I was thirsty and could have used a good cold soda. I did find a cold drink machine, bought an Orange Slice, and poured it down in a second. I walked to a shade tree, the only spot in the park that seemed abandoned. I sat down on the grass under the tree, swallowed the last of the cool soda, and observed the people around me.

There was a five-generation family at a picnic table a few feet away from my serene spot under the shade tree. There was a couple in their eighties apparently celebrating their anniversary. They sat at the table with a cake before them, and I could hear sounds of their joy, laughter, joking. There was another couple—probably in their sixties—grilling steaks, burgers, and hot dogs. The woman must have been the older lady's daughter, because she had a striking resemblance to her. There were other couples in their forties and thirties, and there was another group of college-age people mixed in with teenagers. The teenagers took great interest in playing with the younger children and infants. There were about forty people there celebrating.

I looked at the oldest couple and thought that they must have been together for over fifty years. I wondered how many times that old man must have made the woman angry. How many times has he made her laugh? How many times has she pouted? I decided that whatever had gone on, it had been special. I could tell by the way they looked at each other. They shared a strong bond.

I looked to the other side and spotted a much younger couple, both of whom seemed to be about twenty-five. The husband and wife had their two young children with them. The young baby cried while the father held her and tried to pacify her. The mother was grilling burgers while the toddler stood behind her. They were a happy family celebrating the Fourth of July.

There were others, many others, walking hand in hand, throwing frisbees, playing ball, jumping rope, fishing in the pond, and dancing. I wondered how many people were there at the park because of tradition. We are creatures of habit and tradition. We go to the park to celebrate the Fourth of July, a family day, with an agenda of family festivities. Suddenly I felt angry and then envious. Didn't I want this—a husband, a baby, a family of my own? I wanted to celebrate holidays and anniversaries and have grandchildren, but what do I have? Nothing but a bad attitude. I wanted to crash the picnic, turn over the grills, steal the hamburgers. Hell, I wanted to scream, but what good would that do? Other than get me some free tickets to the nutcracker's suite.

I stretched out under the tree. A million thoughts seemed to roll around in my head until finally there was sleep. I awoke hours later, attacked by a frisbee thrown by an amateur player of five. For a few seconds I was disoriented, paralyzed by this great family gathering. I wondered if I was dreaming, but consciousness gradually brought it all back. I was in the park alone on the Fourth of July, and I had three miles of walking, jogging, running, crawling, or whatever it took before I would be back home.

Deep green grass stains were conspicuous on the back of my pants, my hair had pieces of leaves and grass in it, and I itched all over from chigger bites.

I stood up slowly, brushing the grass and dirt away and preparing myself for the walk back. I wished for cool water to wash my face, but there was none.

Many people had already abandoned the park, and as I walked past the overflowing garbage cans of empty bottles, cans, and morsels of food from the holiday feast, I got a sharp sense that the people had actually been there, that I hadn't dreamed them up.

My walk home was terrible. I feared it would get completely dark before I made it back, and it almost did. The sun was almost completely gone when I turned the key and saw a note from Mark under my door. It read, "I came by."

Some two hours later, fireworks were going off and sporadically lighting up the dark sky. Firecrackers popped like popcorn, and my telephone rang, but I wouldn't answer. I was afraid it was Mark, and afraid I would reconsider and reconcile; afraid to be lonely, and afraid to wreck my life. The telephone rang in fifteen minute intervals for a couple of hours. I did not dare take the receiver off the hook, for fear he would come back.

I took my empty shell of a body to bed with the phone still ringing, reverberating through my apartment. The thought kept running loose in my mind that I must be cracking.

Today, I woke and went through the routine of getting ready and catching the bus. The MTA bus driver made a pass at me, but I ignored him. I got to work on time. Jane and Thomas were not at work, so Phyllis, Jimmy, David, and I carried on with our labels and talked about the festivities of the Fourth. Tomorrow we will finish the labels for sure, and I'm glad. I really don't think I can take much more of sticking labels on envelopes.

July 22
Thursday, 4:00 A.M.

I have done something different at work for the past two weeks. I was separated from the group and sent to work in Appeals under Mr. Calhoun. Appeals deals with those unemployment claims that were filed and denied, then appealed by the claimant. During an appeal, a referee gathers information about the circumstances leading to the claimant's unemployment. The referee may request the claimant's presence at the time of the appeals hearing, or ask for witnesses, the employer, or attorneys to attend the hearing. After the hearing, the referee has to write up a summary and mail out a decision.

My job, along with two other people, was to edit the summaries and decisions. This job requires a quiet, serene atmosphere, and I've missed the laughter of the group and the radio music. Mr. Calhoun is a tall white man in his mid forties with curly auburn hair, pink skin, and a pot-shaped stomach. He was strict in operating his department. We couldn't talk very much or make many personal telephone calls. Tardiness was a cardinal sin.

It has taken every ounce of my strength to get to work by 8:00 every single day. A few days I've actually nodded off while editing reports. Anyway, one funny thing did happen. One of the reports I was editing had the appeals claim in it. The claimant was asked why he appealed the initial decision. He wrote in big block letters: BECAUSE I FEEL THE DECISION WAS IGNORANT! This struck me as funny, and I laughed and grinned to myself for a while.

Tomorrow I will go to do taxes. I don't know what that will involve at this point. It has been a while since I've recorded, and now as I write, I try to recall all the recent events in my life.

Oh, two days after the Fourth holiday, Angela King, one of Mark's many girlfriends, called. I asked how she got the number, but it was obvious that she had somehow gotten it from Mark. She started to cry, saying she had planned to go back to Texas with him, but that he had left her. Did she expect me to feel sorry for her? Please!

She asked me whether it was true that I had filed for a divorce. I told her my concerns were my business, and as for him leaving her, that's the breaks. I hung up the telephone and had a good laugh, and then it hit me. I was so thankful I had not given in to Mark when he had kept calling. He would have made an ass out of me, but I didn't give in to him this time. I really can't believe anything he says, although I think he believes his own lies. He would make a good actor.

I went back to my lawyer on Saturday, and he suggested filing under the Desertion Act. I told him I didn't give a damn if it took an act of Congress, any act that would get me and Mark untied legally was fine with me.

I've talked to Valerie twice since the holiday. She was upset that I didn't come to her house on the Fourth. But apparently she had enough company already with in-laws and some of her other relatives visiting.

98

I called Georgia, but she wasn't home. I left a message on her answering machine. Georgia never stays at home anymore.

I hear noises upstairs. It's not a man after all, but a woman who has moved into the upstairs apartment. Her boyfriend spends nights with her. I get the impression he's a married man, because he never shows up until after dark and usually leaves early in the morning about the time my alarm goes off at 5:30.

July 31
Saturday, 8:00 P.M.

I worked today so that we could complete the taxes. The group—Phyllis, Thomas, Jane, David, Jimmy, and myself—were all back together again. Phyllis still carries her radio and plays country music. We were all seated at a long table, and each person had three boxes in which to file materials.

We had to open mail and separate tax checks from other papers and file them away in boxes. All businesses in the state are required to send in taxes on a quarterly basis, and those taxes not postmarked by the end of the month are penalized.

I have opened long trays of mail, filed papers, and I've had checks of large sums and small sums in my hands today. Hundreds of thousands of dollars have passed through my hands today.

I got paid yesterday, and after paying my bills, I have $67 left to last for two more weeks until my next payday.

Chapter Eight: August

August 6
Saturday, 1:00 P.M.

We finished taxes, and on Monday Jewel Brown, another new employee, and I will be moved to Auditing. I'm not sure just yet what we will be auditing.

Jewel is a short young woman of twenty-one years. She is smaller than I am and weighs only ninety-five pounds. She looks like a child. Her hair is short and tightly curled. She has beautiful brown skin and a pretty smile that shows her dimples.

Jewel started work on Wednesday, and by Thursday we were already getting to be friends. She's a student at the University, majoring in engineering, and she has one more semester before she completes her bachelor's degree. She won't be returning to school this fall because the last two courses required for graduation won't be offered until the spring semester. She confided in me that her plan is to work until December and then go back to school.

Jewel wears a diamond solitaire that she just got a month ago from her boyfriend. They are planning to be married next June, and she has already started preparing for the wedding. She's working and saving her money for expenses. She's planning a big wedding for the day after her graduation. She wants a long white gown with a chapel-length train, groomsmen in tuxedos, six bridesmaids in peach dresses, and a six-tier cake with two large bells on top and a fountain with flowing pink champagne.

It sounded lovely the way she described it, and she brings her *Bride's* magazine to work with her every day. Her fiancé also has an engineering degree from Morehouse in Atlanta, Georgia, which will become their home.

Jewel already has a job lined up with an engineering firm in Atlanta after graduation. She has everything all planned. After they get married, she'll work five years, do some traveling for a year, then get off the pill and start their family. They want two children spaced two years apart, and when they reach school age, Jewel will re-enter the work force. Her fiancé is now shopping around for a house, and at Christmas she'll visit so they can pick their furnishings. They both are Catholic, so their children will attend Catholic school.

She doesn't want to have a maid—Jewel prefers cleaning her own house—but a cook she would welcome, especially since she'll be working the first five years. They want to live in a racially mixed neighborhood or community, and she and her fiancé plan to share the responsibility of managing their money.

It seems they've covered a lot of important concerns before marriage. I listened to all she had to say as she talked eagerly and confidently, as so many new brides and brides-to-be do. I wanted to tell her that nothing works out just as you plan it, but I didn't want to burst her bubble, so I kept my mouth shut and let her enjoy herself.

I got a letter from my brother Sam. It's unusual to get a letter from him, so I ripped the envelope open, and a $100 bill fell out as I unfolded the letter that Rosie, Sam's wife, had written. She wrote that they are planning to visit at the end of the month and will stay for the weekend and go to the fair that's in town. Tony and Timmy, their twin boys, are twelve years old now and are eagerly looking forward to the visit. I marked my calendar and tucked the much-needed hundred dollar bill in my billfold, and then I wrote a letter to Sam and Rosie welcoming them.

August 13
Friday, 7:00 P.M.

My fingers are numb because I've spent my entire week adding up long columns of figures on a calculator. We had to total the columns and be sure they balanced, and any figures that were more than $500 off were to be brought to the attention of the supervisor.

During my lunch hour each day this past week, I have gone window shopping with Jewel and listened to her talk about the wedding. It was refreshing to get out, because this job is boring as hell. We both agree it is not fulfilling our intellectual ability. It's a temporary thing for Jewel, anyway, and I know I have to start looking for something else soon. I do feel just a tinge of guilt about wanting to find another job, because so many people can't get jobs at all, and here I am wanting a new one already. But hell, I'm still barely making ends meet; as a matter of fact, ends *aren't* meeting. I'm having to rob Peter to pay Paul. I'm living from paycheck to paycheck. God only knows what would happen if all the paychecks in America were burned. People wouldn't be able to put gas in their cars or buy food. Hell, what about life without credit cards? Just suppose there were no credit cards, and everything had to be purchased with cash. Imagine spending $60,000 cash for a house or $8,000 cash for a car. I know people used to manage without credit. I mean, in the beginning there was no credit, no mortgage, no bank card, and people slept and rested well at night. Then came lay-a-ways, bank loans, credit, and more credit, and these days you have to have credit to get credit. There's no wonder the new generation and some of the old folk smoke pot and sniff glue. Anything to get away from this plastic world of make-believe.

The average American couple has two cars, three televisions, cable, two living rooms, two refrigerators, three bedrooms, two children, and a dog or a cat, all purchased with plastic. Let's face it: plastic is ingrained into the threads of our society. What was once a luxury is now a necessity, a way of life.

The other evening, some man called here selling burial plots over the phone. He said he picked my number at random. Now they have cemetery plots purchased with plastic. This plastic business has gone too far. I mean, I know you can buy empires with plastic, but a burial plot? Even the dead can't rest in peace anymore. How would you collect from a dead person, anyway? I mean, really.

August 27
Friday, 6:00 P.M.

The past two weeks of work have been total boresville. I would have to be an idiot or a mental midget if I didn't catch on to taking staples out of paper. Over the past three days, that's what I've done, and it's enough to drive a person to drinking. Jewel has helped keep things sort of lively. Yesterday she told me to slow down because I was moving too fast, snapping the little metal clips out like an expert. She said this work is so mentally challenging that she was afraid I would get burnt out. She then smiled and said, "You keep that up, and you might get promoted to supervisor or something." We both had a hearty laugh.

Next week Jewel and I will be separated. I'll be doing some typing and filing, and she'll go back to taxes. But we'll still meet for lunch and run through the bridal sections of the department stores.

Tonight I am expecting my brother and his family to arrive around 8:00. I did some grocery shopping after work, and I guess I'd better start preparing the meal.

August 28
Saturday, 9:00 a.m.

Last night was interesting. I put the turnip greens, squash, and fried chicken on about 7:00. This was the first complete meal I've prepared since I moved into this apartment. As I prepared the food and smelled the various aromas, I felt nostalgic for a few minutes. I thought about how it used to be when I would rush home and stir the pots and pans for Mark. Now I eat incomplete meals. I mean, it's kind of senseless to prepare a big meal for one person.

Maybe it really is true that life is meant to be shared, preferably with a person that wants to share, too. People are supposed to be paired off, aren't they? I mean, didn't Noah take two of each animal on the ark? This society is geared toward couples and legal partnerships. People who shack up are frowned upon. I don't know if it's wrong or right anymore, because if people who are legally married don't take their marriage vows seriously, then what do they really have, other than a glorified shack job? And if two people are shacking up, and they're truly committed to the relationship, then why wouldn't they want to sign the papers to show the seriousness of their commitment? This makes my head hurt, because there's no cut and dried answer.

Anyway, at about 8:30, Sam, Rosie, and the twins arrived. Sam and Rosie have been married for a long time, and their birthdays are on the same day. They were married for a few years before Rosie got pregnant and had the twins. They had started talking about adopting because they were getting discouraged, but as soon as they did, Rosie got pregnant, and Tony and Timmy were born under Gemini, the sign of the twins. They're identical twins.

Sam and Rosie have been living in Toledo, Ohio for years. Sam started a janitorial service there, and Rosie was his business manager. Then she started reading up on investments, and they purchased several old apartment complexes and renovated them for renting. They're doing pretty well, but that Rosie is still as money conscious

105

and penny-pinching as ever. Sam tried to get me to go to college in Toledo, but I just didn't want to live there.

The twins take after our side of the family. They're tall boys, and they have Sam's facial features. I have not seen them in at least four years. They love to kid, joke, and play tricks on people. The little scoundrels had on identifying T-shirts. One said, "Hi, I'm Tony, he's Timmy," and the other one said the reverse. I thought this was a clever idea. But they grinned at each other every time I called their names. I noticed that when I addressed Tony, Timmy answered, and vice versa. Sam was about to pop after an hour of it and finally made the boys confess. They had traded T-shirts. I had a good laugh about it, and then we set the table and ate dinner.

We were up until 2:00 this morning laughing and talking. Sam requested cabbage, neck bones, fried apples, and hot water cornbread for supper tomorrow.

I really thought that my eyelids would be stuck together this morning, but surprisingly I woke early and felt energized. It must be the excitement of having guests.

I hear movements in the apartment, so my guests must be awake.

August 29
Sunday, 8:30 P.M.

I think I slept for about six hours last night. I can certainly tell that I'm aging, but this time my guests helped me along. Yesterday the four of them begged me to go to the fair with them. I said I thought it should be a family outing, and Sam let me have it. He said, "It sure is, and you're a part of this family. Or did you forget that, Little Sister?"

The twins kept on begging. "Come on, Aunt Norma Jean, please come with us!"

I mentioned that supper would still have to be cooked, but Rosie quickly stepped in. "Girl, it will not take all day to fix cabbage and chime bones, so come on!"

Well, it was four against one, so I couldn't win and really didn't feel like fighting that hard. I rode in the back seat of the car with the twins and gave Sam directions to the fairgrounds.

The twins had brought their cameras with them. Timmy had his ready, but Tony still struggled with trying to get the film loaded in his. After finishing that task, they relaxed and let the talk drift back to their home in Ohio. They told me about their dog, Mister, and wondered if the neighbor had remembered to feed him. I could tell both of them were quite fond of Mister, and as it turned out, they had already had a total of four dogs in their twelve years. The first one was a female dog, a German shepherd they called Mrs. She was killed by a car. Then they had another female dog, a collie named Lady. Lady loved ice cream and daisies. She died after eating some poison someone put down. Then they had a male Doberman named Duke, and he was either stolen or wandered off. And of course, now they have Mister, a male boxer. By the time we reached the fairgrounds, I knew the family's entire dog history. It was ninety degrees in the shade, and the fairgrounds were packed. After we entered the gate, Sam purchased a booklet that contained maps and illustrations of the grounds.

There were several exhibits to visit, and all the lines were exceptionally long. The sun didn't pity us either, and it didn't take long for my blouse to look like I'd been in a baptism. After the seventh exhibit, I quit counting, because it was just too hot and none of the stuff was very interesting. Sam and Rosie looked pretty bored as well, but Tony and Timmy loved it. They talked about the model set-ups like experts. Tony explained the solar energy exhibit and was totally talking over my head. I wondered if these twins were exceptionally bright, or if I was just getting stupid. Rosie must have sensed my exasperation, because she pulled me to one side and said, "Norma Jean, the boys are good readers, and they're in special classes at school. They're gifted and do especially well in the sciences. Don't worry, most of the time I don't know what they're talking about, either! They're just so clever. It's not easy rearing a couple of smart alecks!" We both laughed at this. She gazed at the two of them, now several feet ahead of us. "I love those two little devils. I haven't said anything before about their being gifted, because they're modest. They say they don't want to be treated any differently than anyone else, and I try to keep it that way."

We hastened our pace and caught up with Sam and the twins. Tony was saying that he wanted to be a chemical engineer, and Timmy said he wanted to be an astronomer. Then, as we were walking side by side, Timmy turned to me and asked, "Did you know if a person could travel at the speed of light, he could leave right this instant and travel the distance of the earth, and he'd be back before you could blink an eye? As a matter of fact, you wouldn't even know he had gone."

Tony laughed and said, "That's what you call being back before you know it!" All five of us chuckled.

We must have walked about twenty miles all over the fairgrounds. Rosie bought lots of souvenirs, but I only bought one thing. It was a cigarette and a match encased in glass, and on the outside it read, "In case of emergency, break glass." I thought this was an appropriate souvenir, because it would help me remember the fair as well as the fact that I quit smoking. Anyway, we got back to the apartment after dark, and we didn't have any cabbage and neck bones. Our stomachs were already too full with hot dogs and sodas.

I got up early this morning and did some grocery shopping, and by noon the cabbage dinner was prepared. We all ate together, and by 1:00 Sam and his family were packed up, heading for Crossroads where they planned to spend three or four days with Mama.

I was more lonely after they left. You really don't realize the difference it makes having someone around until you're alone again. This apartment was so quiet, it was depressing. Then I suddenly remembered that Sam had brought a fifth of Jack Daniel's whiskey with him, and over three-fourths was left. I got the bottle of whiskey, put two ice cubes in a glass, and poured myself a stiff drink. I gulped that stuff down like water, and seconds later I had a woozy feeling, and my throat felt hot. I think it took me about thirty minutes to pass out, and I woke up only minutes ago. I smell like liquor. My bedroom smells like liquor. The empty glass is on my nightstand, and I'm tempted to drink another glass, except that my head is throbbing.

I am going to take tomorrow off. It's my thirty-second birthday, and I'm going to celebrate it, even if I have to do it alone.

August 30
Monday, 10:00 P.M.

Happy Birthday To Me! Only one person has wished me a happy birthday today, and that was my Mama. She called very early this morning.

I've been thinking the entire day about what this birthday business really means. Let's see, thirty-two years ago on this day, Mama was having labor pains. She was at home, and an elderly midwife helped to bring me into the world. In my thirty-two years of life, I've managed to finish high school and college, become a member of the Baptist faith, write ninety-eight poems that never got published, travel to ten different states, work eight different jobs, get married, get almost divorced, and drink one-half bottle of Jack Daniel's whiskey. Not bad for thirty-two years. At the rate I'm going I might even move into a decent apartment and buy a new car by the time I am thirty-three, or maybe I'll be promoted to supervisor at work.

I can remember having only two birthday parties in my entire life. The first one was when I turned ten, and I invited all my schoolmates. The second party was when I was fourteen. At both parties, I got birthday spankings, including the extra whop which was supposed to be "one to grow on."

Today I didn't have a gathering, but I've been drinking this liquor all day. I certainly can't give myself the birthday spanking, but I can say one thing is for certain—this year has really been the one to grow on.

On that note, I am going to bed so that I can make it to work tomorrow.

Chapter Nine: September

September 4
Saturday, 4:30 P.M.

Right this minute I feel sick to my stomach. It's a combination of my hangover from all the whiskey I have been drinking and my heartsick feeling that the world is not real, that my sense of reality was never real.

Life is never simple, not for me. There are so many things that can deter our plans, so many unforeseen circumstances and factors that affect our destiny. Even as I write this, there are forces I don't know about that are affecting my future.

When you really think about it, the odds of being born and growing up a physically and mentally healthy individual and becoming a productive person in society are very slim. For one thing, birth itself is traumatic. Being pushed from the safe environment of our mother's womb out into the world with its wide open spaces and many dangers is threatening to say the least. If we're lucky, we're born into this world, adapt and adjust, and we grow into healthy individuals with goals and plans to help us live out our days as productive people. But sometimes I think life is like that for very few people.

I feel terrible today. When I returned to work on Tuesday, August 31, I was feeling deflated—I'm a year older and have gotten nowhere. At lunch Jewel asked me to go with her to the stores to window shop, but I really didn't feel like it, so I told her I didn't feel well. She left at noon, but she didn't make it back to work. At 2:00 I wondered where she was, because it's unlike her to be tardy. Around 3:15, we got the message that Jewel was at Lakeside Hospital in a coma. Apparently she had gone window shopping and then decided to purchase something for the wedding. Unfortunately, the store clerk had waxed the floor, which was slick and shiny. On top of that someone had spilled something that hadn't been mopped up. Jewel paid for her items, made five steps toward the door, and slipped. She was caught off guard, and her hands were full, so she couldn't catch herself. She had an awful fall on the hard concrete floor and bumped her head. Apparently she got a concussion. According to the policeman, Jewel was talking initially and breathing without difficulty, but then she lost consciousness. I called her physician later, and he said Jewel had a severe fall but that her vital signs were stable. However, she was not responding to much, and he said the next twenty-four hours were critical. Jewel's fiancé flew in from Atlanta, and her parents came. I am praying for her.

September 10
Friday, 6:30 P.M.

This week has been a struggle. I have already consumed two bottles of liquor, and I realized today that I'll be on a path of destruction if I don't stop this drinking now before it gets out of hand. I have drunk more liquor in the past few days than I drank in all of last year. I know this isn't right.

I do feel better about Jewel, though. She's out of intensive care. She's conscious, but she's having some tingling sensations in her legs.

When she first regained consciousness, she couldn't speak. But she was aware of her surroundings and could move her fingers and arms. I visited with her that day and read her poems and get well cards. She seemed like she wanted to say something and kept looking over at the nightstand. So I opened her nightstand drawer and took out some tissues, but her glance told me instantly that was not what she wanted. Then I saw her *Bride's* magazine. I pulled it out of the drawer and held it in front of her, and her eyes just danced. I turned the pages one by one so that she could see them. When I got to the page with the wedding dress she had chosen, she started to cry, so I closed the magazine and put it back in the drawer. I hugged and kissed her and told her everything would be all right. She squeezed my hand and relaxed, and before I left, she was fast asleep.

This entire ordeal has been terrible. All I can think about is Jewel. It's so unfair. She was so excited about her upcoming marriage, and now this happens.

On Labor Day night, around 11:00, the police visited my apartment. They said they had a warrant for Mark's arrest. It seems Mark wrote some bad checks when he was in town on the Fourth of July, apparently from our old, closed-out joint bank account. I explained to the officers that we were separated and that divorce proceedings had already begun. They told me they would have to have my lawyer's name and number, so I wrote it down for them. One officer also informed me that there is some suspicion that Mark is involved in drug trafficking. They left after about thirty minutes and said they would check out my story with my attorney, and if it didn't work out, they would be back.

My nerves were shot to hell, so I poured myself a drink before the flashing blue lights turned the corner. It's really strange how just knowing someone or having been married to someone can cause so much hurt and pain, even after the ties have been severed. The ghost of the relationship comes back to haunt you, almost like an eternal shadow—not always visible, but on certain days, just as conspicuous as the nose on your face. I cursed the day I met Mark.

On Tuesday the seventh, I made it in to work. I'm sure I looked like I had a hangover, and I felt nauseous the entire day. When I got home from work, Carmen came over to tell me she had graduated from LPN training. I was happy for her and told her so. She was in good spirits because she'd also hit the numbers. I think I've played the numbers maybe twice in my life and didn't win anything. But Carmen felt like she was on a roll. "There's another hot number due to fall any day," she said. "It's 854. You should put some change on it, Norma."

"Where?" I asked.

She said, "Girl, you don't know nothing. You got a number runner living right over your head! The girl that moved upstairs, her old man, Tap, is a number runner. He picks the numbers up every morning about 5:30 or 6:00." I thanked Carmen for enlightening me.

On Wednesday morning I put fifty cents on 854, and 983 fell. On Thursday, I don't why I did it, but I put twenty cents on 983 even though it fell the day before. And bingo! 983 fell again. It's very rare that happens. I collected $150, a much-needed $150. Now I can relax a little, breathe a little.

September 18
Saturday, 4:30 P.M.

Several things have happened over the past week. For one thing, Jewel was discharged from the hospital. She's talking and walking with assistance, and she'll have to get daily physical therapy for a while until she regains complete use of her legs. The doctor thinks it may take a month or two. Her fiancé has been very dedicated. There's no doubt there's going to be a wedding, and there's going to be a law suit, too. The store will probably settle out of court. Jewel is lucky; she's going to be okay and will continue to move forward with her life.

The second thing that happened this week is that on Wednesday I went to court, and my divorce is now final. I'm a free woman, and I have my maiden name back, Norma Jean Harris. My lawyer had the nerve to tell me that if I wanted to remarry, I had to wait thirty days. I laughed in his face. I probably won't marry for another thirty *years*. I'm glad it's over, and I feel good about this divorce.

The third thing is that Mark is in jail in Texas. I got a letter from him asking me for money to help him get out of trouble. I threw it in the trash.

The last thing that happened this week is that Dr. David Monroe called me Wednesday night, almost like he instinctively knew my divorce was final. He said he'd been looking for my number for some time because there was a vacant position at Merci hospital. It was for a patient care representative. "You will be excellent for the job," he said. He suggested that I get an updated resumé printed and meet him on Monday evening at 6:30 at Roger's, an exclusive restaurant. He said he would arrange my interview. We talked for at least an hour.

Things are finally breaking now; my life is going to move in a positive direction for a change. I can feel it. In fact, I feel so good that I'm going to promise myself that I'll never again drink to ease any pain in my life. I refuse to let alcohol be my crutch.

September 20
Monday, 10:17 P.M.

I met Dr. Monroe at 6:30 tonight. He was dressed in a dark, conservative suit. We met in the parking lot, greeted each other, and then entered Roger's together.

We were seated in a nice dinner suite near the pianist, who sang "Moon River" as we were being seated. The pianist apparently took requests as well, because I noticed someone asking him to sing "Misty." Near the pianist was a lady dressed in a long black gown, selling roses.

That restaurant is one of the most expensive in the city. The artwork was nice, the chandeliers and candelabras were so elegant, and even the ladies' room was so breathtakingly beautiful that I could have stayed in there all night. I've never seen anything like it. First of all, the bathroom counters and the doors were black marble, and the doors had mother-of-pearl and abalone designs on the front. By the sink where I washed my hands was a towel girl standing there to hand me a towel. There were bottles and bottles of expensive perfumes if you wanted to freshen up. It was certainly first class.

Dr. Monroe ordered a bottle of white dinner wine, and the waiter, dressed in a black tuxedo, brought it out in a silver ice bucket. This place was gorgeous. I thought I had died and gone to heaven. The menu was divine, and I ordered prime rib with all the trimmings.

We talked, ate, and I drank only one glass of wine. Then he asked me for my resumé, and as he reviewed it, he kept nodding his head and finally said, "Very good." He told me I would have an interview scheduled by Wednesday and should be ready to start work possibly by the fourth of October. The evening was certainly enjoyable, very lovely, and different from any other dinner date I have ever had. I really needed this, because it's been so very long since I have been on a date. He bought me a rose from the lady in the long black dress, and he asked the piano player to sing "Misty" again in my honor. I did not want this evening to end. At 8:00 we parted in the parking lot, with David promising to call me on Tuesday night to confirm the interview date. He said I must call him "David" from now on. I think he's interested.

I'm sort of puzzled, because he really didn't make a pass at me. Usually passes annoy me, but I really wanted him to make one tonight.

Anyway, I'm on cloud nine, and I'm crossing my fingers about the job.

September 27
Monday, 3:30 P.M.

David called me Tuesday night and confirmed the interview for Wednesday.

I dressed carefully for this interview. I wore my navy suit, a white blouse, and navy shoes. I met with Dr. Winston Coleman, the hospital administrator, at 1:30 Wednesday afternoon. Dr. Coleman looked like he could be a hundred years old. His hair was as white as snow, and his hands were really wrinkled. The interview lasted for about thirty minutes. He reviewed my resumé and asked for a copy of my references, which I gave him. Apparently he wanted to make me sweat, because he said he would let me know his decision on Friday.

Sure enough, at Dr. Coleman's request, his secretary phoned me on Friday to tell me I got the job and to report to work on the fourth of October. I immediately informed my present employers—who couldn't have cared less. I gave my written notice and quit the same day, allowing myself a week's vacation prior to starting my new job.

David called me on Friday night, and on Saturday we went to dinner again. This time we went to Chopsticks, a fancy Japanese restaurant. The chef is very entertaining; he prepares your meal right before you. Everyone eats with chop sticks. It was a trip! I kept dropping my food, but I had the hang of it before we left. David still did not make a pass at me. I'm so puzzled! What does he want? I know he's not doing all of this for nothing. Now, that's not to say that I'm not qualified, because I'll do a good job, and I know he believes I will, too. But he wants something, and hell, I could use some! I am so hard up right now I have started having sexy dreams, and those orgasms you have when you're dreaming are like riding a cloud. Anyway, if he doesn't make a move soon, I might have to put a rush on him.

On Sunday I visited Georgia. I was glad to finally catch up with her. She looked better, and I'm sure it's because she's in therapy. She gave me the latest scoop on David. He quit Hillhaven at least two months ago. He's on staff at Merci hospital as well as with the medical group. Business is booming for him, and he's apparently a wise investor. According to Georgia, the man is rolling in dough. She said, "Girl, he asked me for your number a long time ago before he quit Hillhaven, and I've meant to ask you if it was okay, but you know how preoccupied I have been. I just completely forgot."

We talked about a lot of things, but mostly about how crime seems to be escalating, especially among teenagers. I told her I was concerned that these teenage boys really don't have much to do but hang out on street corners and be idle. She said she's not angry now about the robbery and what happened to her. She feels sorry for the young men. She also said she now realizes crime can happen in any neighborhood. It was good seeing Georgia. She's changed, and I think she has become more sensitive to other people.

I visited Jewel, and she's really making positive progress. She nearly talked me to death. She's still limping slightly, but her physical therapy is helping. She and her fiancé are definitely suing the department store. She even joked that she's probably going to end up owning some stock in that company. We talked for a couple of hours, and then I went by Valerie's. Jack got called back to work, and not only is he working his full time job, but he's working an evening job as well. Valerie is working now, too, and she really likes having a career. It's a good diversion from cooking meals and washing clothes. I was satisfied after having seen my friends and finding out that they were well. Tomorrow I am going to start making plans to move.

September 30
Thursday, 8:30 P.M.

Even though I've wanted to, I haven't called David. I just didn't think it would be a good thing to do yet. But then he came by here last night, and he finally made his first move! Apparently he has not figured out that I have the hots for him. He invited me to come over to

118

his condo on Friday evening. He'll pick me up at 7:00. He kissed my lips lightly before he left. I can still feel his lips. I want him pretty damn bad. I hope I don't hurt this man, but I have a mind to give him one hell of a workout!

I have found an apartment on Drew Circle Drive that I really like. It's a two bedroom with a balcony, glass patio doors, a sunken bathtub, and washer and dryer hook-ups. Maybe after I start my new job, I can afford to move into a place like that. Thank God that things really are looking brighter.

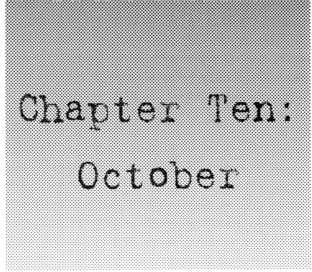

Chapter Ten:
October

October 2
Saturday, 3:15 P.M.

I visited the flea market today for the first time since February. I only bought one thing, and it wasn't depression glass. There was an elderly woman there selling antique jewelry. She had a bracelet with a black leather band and silver coiled around a rainbow crystal on the top. She told me about the healing power of crystals, how they can bring you peace, serenity, and happiness if used in the right way. So I bought the bracelet.

Speaking of happiness, I believe David is good luck for me. He is so supportive and encouraging. I've never met or dated a man with such confidence. He doesn't feel threatened by me, and he doesn't have a need to control me. He just wants to make me happy. All I know is I like him, and I like the way he makes me feel so special. I like how he looks, smells, smiles—hell, I even like his attitude.

Well, now about Friday evening. David picked me up around 7:00. He's always on time. We went to another really nice restaurant, one called First Class. It's a French restaurant—the menu was in

French, and the waiters talked with French accents. I had everything from an appetizer of escargot to a fabulous dessert. I really think David is trying to fatten me up. I've already gained ten pounds, and I'm definitely going to gain more if I keep hanging around with him. We finished dinner, left around 9:00, and went to his boat. I've never been on a boat before in my entire life. The moon shining on the water at night is lovely. We laughed and talked, mostly about me. David was full of questions, and I had diarrhea of the mouth. I felt so comfortable with him, like I had known him all my life. We stayed on the boat for an hour and then drove to his condo in the suburbs. It was a lovely place, beautifully decorated. David pulled out some of his jazz albums and tapes—and also some oldies but goodies—and we drank one glass of wine together. When we finished the wine, we started to dance, at first to fast, up-beat music, and then to a slow song. Then he put the Isley Brothers' "Choosy Lover" on, and in the middle of the song, he squeezed me and blew in my ear, and it sent chills down my spine. I got eager and kissed him, and he kissed me back, and then I was unbuttoning his shirt and unzipping his pants. He slowly unbuttoned my blouse, and then we undressed each other down to the last stitch of clothing. We were still dancing, both of us naked, with all of our clothing on the floor around our bare feet. The music played softly as we blended and melted into each other, more and more with each rhythmic beat. He said, "You are so beautiful. I have always wanted you, from the very first time I laid eyes on you." When neither one of us could take it any longer, he had me right there in the middle of the floor, on the thick plush carpet. I was swept away in a whirl of passion such as I have never known before. I spent the night, and before morning, we were making love again, this time upstairs in his king-sized bed.

Before Mark, when I had sex with a guy, we were just screwing around. With Mark, the sex was great, but it was empty. With David, I was making love. It was great.

David has hooked me, because now I want him. I crave his body, and I want his mind and heart, and it seems that he craves mine as well. I'm getting excited just writing about him. I think David is ripe for the picking.

October 3
Sunday, 4:00 P.M.

David came by today, and guess what happened. His animal magnetism drove me wild. When I'm with him, I want to do things for him. I can't do enough, and I've never felt this way before. I even got my oils and creams out and heated them and gave him a massage.

Anyway, now I feel relaxed, satisfied, and ready to start the new job tomorrow. I think my decision to take the week off before starting my new job was a good one. I really needed the time.

Getting back to David, the other day, I asked him if he'd ever been married. Of course I knew he hadn't, but I didn't want him to know I was so well informed. He said no, he never married, and he looked kind of sad. He told me something I'm sure he doesn't talk about very often. David is the son of a farmer in a rural Mississippi county. He was the seventh of fourteen children, and they were dirt poor. David didn't have money, but he had books, and he enjoyed reading. At age ten he decided he was going to be a doctor.

David's first love was a girl named Lois Ann Holiway, a tall, thin girl with light brown skin and shoulder-length hair. She was the prettiest black girl in the county. David liked her a lot, and he respected her. Lois Ann's parents were educated—her father was a principal, and her mother was the school guidance counselor. Lois Ann had a younger brother, and because it was just the two of them, Lois Ann got whatever she wanted. She took piano lessons, voice lessons, and dance classes. Her parents didn't approve of David. They felt he was too poor, too black, and going nowhere. They called him a descendent of field hands. They did everything within their power to discourage their daughter's relationship with him. They never really talked with David or asked him about his own personal ambitions.

Shortly after high school, Lois Ann married Reverend Clayton's son, Joseph. She was three months pregnant when they married, and the entire town knew it. Well, Joseph became a minister like his father, and now he pastors one of the largest Baptist churches in that part of Mississippi. They have eight children and are still together. David said that experience hurt him and messed with his self esteem. But it made him even more determined to succeed. He graduated from college and went on to medical school, and then he started his own medical practice. He worked night and day for ten years, and he invested in real estate, stocks, bonds, money market certificates, certificates of deposits, Jinny Mae's, and T-Bills—you name it. He said he was obsessed with working, making money, and having his money work for him. In the meantime, women were coming and going in his life like musical chairs, some black, some white, some oriental. But none of them seemed to fill the void he felt. Then about five years ago, when he turned forty, he decided he would be very selective about the women he dated. He decided that just any woman, just any pretty face, wouldn't do. He said he was emotionally void, tired of feeling numb, and he wanted to feel anticipation and excitement about a relationship. He said he never felt that energy until the day he met me. He said, "The first time I saw you, there was something about you that made me realize that you were the one. But you were a married woman then, getting ready to move to another state with your husband. I had just met you, and you were leaving in two weeks. Remember that? I bet you never gave me a second thought. You looked happy and ready to join your husband, and since I'm not in the habit of breaking up marriages, I never made a move. But when I saw you again at the hospital, visiting your friend—what's her name? Georgia?—I wanted to say something then, but I realized that the time wasn't right. You were naturally upset over your broken marriage and your job situation. I knew I had to wait until you were ready. Anyway, after getting your number, I felt the right time would come. One thing I know is that you're a lovely person in flesh and in spirit, and I'm so glad that everything has worked out."

When David explained all that, he helped me to understand why he was so patient, why he waited so long. He's a very perceptive person.

David left after that, promising to call me early in the morning to awaken me and wish me luck on my first day at work at Merci hospital.

I feel so good. Everything is finally coming together. Thank God for the bitter and the sweet. I know one thing: maybe that lady at the flea market was right about those crystals.

October 4
Monday, 8:15 P.M.

It has been a busy day. First of all, David phoned me this morning at 6:00. I was already up and in the bathtub. I took my time getting ready for work. I even prepared a light breakfast of toast, hard boiled eggs, and a glass of juice. I left the apartment at 7:30 and arrived at Merci Hospital at 7:50. I didn't have a parking sticker, so I had to park in the pay lot. I'd been instructed to report to hospital personnel at 8:00, and I met with the personnel director, Mr. Cheatham, an attractive man in his mid-thirties. I signed my W-4 forms and my salary agreement. The position pays enough for me to pay my bills and actually have some left over for extras. Mr. Cheatham reviewed the hospital policy about holidays, vacation time, sick days, the pay schedule, insurance benefits, their credit union, and so forth. At 9:15, I met with Adam Carter, the staff psychologist. He deals specifically with employees' personal and work-related problems. Then I had my identification picture taken, and I was instructed to wear it at all times during work hours. After that, I was given a white lab coat to wear any time I went on the service floors. Then I went on a tour of the hospital, which consisted of medicine, surgery, ob/gyn, pediatrics and the nursery, and geriatrics. At noon I had an hour lunch break. I went to the cafeteria with Mrs. Johnson, my tour guide.

The cafeteria was crowded with people in white lab coats and white uniforms. I could hear the intercom system behind the chatter of the doctors, interns, nurses, and other hospital personnel. Then I heard a page for Dr. David Monroe. I hadn't seen David all day. After lunch I went to get my automobile sticker, and they told me the parking fee is $7.00 every two weeks. At 1:45 I met with Miss Wiggins, the business office manager. She introduced me to the staff and described the business aspects of the hospital. It seems they get a lot of medicare and medicaid recipients here, and lots of indigent patients, too. The indigent patients usually go through emergency and are labeled "dire emergency," meaning they're either in need of blood or oxygen, or it's a case of life or death. After the session with Miss Wiggins, I went to meet the cafeteria staff, and here I met the head dietician, Mrs. Katie James, a thin, wiry white woman in her mid-fifties. She explained the process of planning diets and how they're ordered. Then I went to the social services department, and right away I felt some interesting vibes. The director of social services, Mrs. Marcia Taylor, is a slightly pudgy white woman of medium height with shoulder-length, fire-red hair and freckles on her face. She had a southern accent and introduced herself and told me about the department. She supervises a staff of six workers, five women and one man. One black woman was in the group, and it was so obvious there was some long-standing friction there. Mrs. Taylor even spoke of the black woman with a different tone of voice. I knew there was hostility, but I couldn't figure out why.

I met the six workers one by one. Martin Jefferson, the only man in the group, is probably in his late twenties. He's a tall, thin white man with shy eyes like blue marbles and a neatly trimmed mustache. He gave me a friendly "hello" that showed off his New England accent.

The other four women were like clones. If you've seen one, you have seen them all. They're all short, slightly stocky white women dressed in shift-made dresses, and all of them are in their thirties or forties.

I finally met Freda Avery, the other black woman in the department. She's a short, tiny, dainty person, and she was dressed in the prettiest outfit, a burnt orange suit with beige accessories. The orange complimented her yellow skin tone nicely. She had just a tinge of rouge on her high cheekbones and a touch of color on her lips. I thought she could have easily been a model.

Freda's probably in her mid-thirties. She's divorced and doesn't have any children. She was married to a white man, a middle class, mid-western resident doctor with a roaming eye. They came to Merci Hospital when he started the residency program here. Freda was hired at Merci a few months after they moved here, and since she had kept her maiden name when she married him, many people here never knew she was his wife. But once her coworkers learned she was married to a white man—a doctor at that—some of them were pissed. There was conflict at work and at social gatherings, and eventually they found a way to split up Freda and her husband, mainly by playing on his weakness for other women. They fixed him up with white women behind Freda's back, and her marriage fell apart. Their divorce had become final three years ago, and Dr. Townsend had left town with his blonde bride-to-be, while Freda stayed behind and kept her social work job, their $350,000 home, $1000 per month in alimony, and the Mercedes. The white coworkers that had caused all the trouble now liked her even less. And some of her black coworkers didn't like her either. They had labeled her a white man's woman and would have nothing to do with her, especially after her divorce when she wouldn't date black men.

Freda is not a passive woman. She definitely knows how to speak up for herself. Her good looks have helped her win favors and get the things she wanted.

After learning all of this, I still felt that something else must have happened between Freda and Mrs. Taylor. There was a specific hostility between them that seemed different, more personal.

At 4:30 I left work. It had been an action-packed day, and I still had a folder full of materials to read before tomorrow. I got home around 5:00 and rested a while before dinner. Tomorrow I'll visit the various wards and services and meet some of the nursing staff.

David called me at 7:00 to ask about my day. "It was certainly different," I told him.

I must start preparing for tomorrow.

October 5
Tuesday, 10:00 P.M.

Today was Mama's birthday, and I called her bright and early. I had sent her a dozen red roses and a card. She was delighted and said she had gotten the roses yesterday.

Now on a different note, I'm keyed up from work today and the excitement that went on. One of the resident doctors has been accused of murdering his wife! It's hard to believe. Everyone at the hospital was talking about it today. R. D. Johns, the doctor in question, came home and found his wife in bed with another woman. Seeing the two of them being intimate apparently caused him to go temporarily insane, and he picked up a lamp and beat his wife to death. Although she was injured, the other woman managed to escape. Dr. Johns was arrested soon after, and it's rumored that he was then taken to Hillhaven for psychiatric evaluation and treatment. The news made the front page of the paper, and there have been frequent T.V. reports, too. Rumor also has it that Freda was a friend of Dr. John's wife. I also heard today that Freda was actually fired six months ago. But the director cited too many personal reasons for firing her and couldn't really justify the action with any inadequate work performance or violations on Freda's part. So Freda's attorney had a field day, and she was back to work in two months, before she'd even used all of her vacation time.

Freda's victory and her return to work made Mrs. Taylor nauseous with anger, hostility, and contempt for Freda. That must be why there are such bad vibes between them.

I heard enough gossip today to write a soap opera. For instance, Dr. Coleman, the administrator who interviewed me, was caught with his administrative assistant giving him a blow job. Now, what I'm wondering is how in this world she found his shriveled-up dick among all those wrinkles! There must be a ton of wrinkles down there, as old as that man is. I swear, *General Hospital* has nothing on this place.

October 12
Tuesday, 8:09 P.M.

I visited the medical unit today. There are approximately forty patients on this floor. The head nurse, Mrs. Harper, is an amazon of a woman with black hair and blue eyes. She looks very matronly.

I visited all of the patients on the floor. Most of them are senior citizens, and some are so old and disabled they didn't even notice me when I peeked into their rooms. One thing I learned immediately about those who are alert is that they're starved for attention and affection. They were so lonely, and some of them nearly talked me to death. They were so sweet and cute. The last visit I made was with a lady named Mrs. Appleby. She's an eighty-five-year-old terminal cancer patient, and she had tubes, IV needles, and several other things hooked to her body. She never made a movement to show she was aware of my presence. Her husband sat quietly by her bedside, holding her hands. It was obvious that he'd been there all day, because his pants were all wrinkled, and he looked really tired. I introduced myself and asked him how long she had been in the hospital. He looked at me sadly and said, "She's been like this for pretty near two weeks. I know I'm going to lose my Lizzie. The doctors already told me she ain't got long." He teared up. I could tell the old man wanted to talk about it, so I sat down and encouraged him to vent his feelings. Hell, venting your feelings is good for the soul; after all, that's what I'm doing every time I write in this journal. Anyway, the strange thing is that I felt like I knew these people, but from where I couldn't remember. I told him that I knew it had been difficult for him, and he replied, "Me and Lizzie have been married for sixty years. We just had our sixtieth wedding anniversary on the Fourth of July. We've been together so long, I don't think I know how to live without her. We've got children, grandchildren, great-grand children, and great-great-grandchildren. We've outlived two of our own children, three of their children, and one of our great-grandchildren. Me and Lizzie buried our own, and though we knew the day would come and we didn't know who would go first, we always dreaded this time. I really hoped I'd go first, but poor Lizzie took sick after Labor Day and has been going downhill fast. Doctors say her age is against her, and it's out of their hands now. So I just come every day and spend what time I've got left with my Lizzie. You know, me and Lizzie never spent a night apart in our sixty years of marriage."

The old man was struggling with the idea of living alone without his Lizzie. I felt for him, I felt his pain, but I knew I had to give him strength. I told him that it was wonderful that the two of them had lived a long, happy, fulfilling life together, and that so many people don't get that chance. At least he'll have lots of happy memories, and he can thank God that he doesn't have any grudges or guilty feelings toward his wife. After I said that, he perked up a little and dried his eyes. He thanked me for visiting the room, and shortly thereafter, I left. I prayed for him and for his wife and family. I prayed God would take her soon. The agony of watching his wife waste away was killing the old man's spirit. He may as well have been the one in the hospital bed with all the tubes. If it went on much longer, it would probably kill him.

Lizzie Appleby died the next day. It was when I saw Mr. Appleby in the hall being comforted by his children that I realized they were the old couple I saw in the park on the Fourth of July. They didn't know then it would be their last anniversary. I'm glad they had a happy one.

I'm exhausted, so I'd better get to bed.

October 19
Tuesday, 6:30 A.M.

I've received my first paycheck, and it looks good. I think I can start seriously looking for another apartment. But although this seems kind of crazy, I'm gonna miss this place. David and I have been going to dinner a lot lately, and we talk every day. He's been hinting about a surprise I might get around the first part of November. I'm dying to know what it is, but he won't tell me.

October 22
Friday, 10:00 P.M.

I had a nice, exciting experience today at work. It happened this afternoon around 5:30. I had to work late, and on my way out to the garage where my car was parked, who did I see parked in a plain-looking Ford near my car? None other than the singer and enter-tainer, Al Jarreau! He was in a car along with another man and a woman. Hospital security surrounded the car, and there were some other hospital staff members standing around, so I asked one of them what was going on. They said that Al Jarreau was in town performing at the auditorium tonight at 8:00. But he also happens to be on the Board of Trustees of the hospital. Apparently he wanted to drop by for a casual visit with some of the hospital administrators since he had to be in town anyway. I couldn't believe I was close enough to touch him. After they got out of the car, I followed them back into the hospital and waited until Mr. Jarreau's meeting with the adminis-trators was finished. Then I walked right up to him, shook his hand, and told him how much I admired him. Then I asked for his auto-graph. As it happened, the only paper I had with me was my first paycheck stub, so he signed the back of it. I swear I've been hum-ming his songs for the last three hours. I'm going to get this paycheck stub framed.

Ironic as it may be with so much excitement today, today would also have been my sixth wedding anniversary. I feel sorry for Mark, but I can't help him. The only thing I can do is pray for him.

October 24
Sunday, 8:00 P.M.

David told me today that his plans are all arranged, and we'll go to the mountains for the first weekend in November. I'm so excited about it! We'll stay in a log cabin and rest and relax away from civilization. It'll be a treat I really need.

Chapter Eleven:
November

November 8
Monday, 9:00 P.M.

The trip to the mountains was everything I imagined and more. We left on Friday evening. David drove for about seventy miles. We even sang songs along the way. It was so nice to be out on the highway, passing trees with leaves of gold, rust, and burgundy. The scenery was breathtakingly beautiful. David had bought a time share in the cabin where we stayed, and it was made of huge, steady logs and was so comfortable inside. He built a fire in the fireplace, and then we just sat and watched the fire spark and the logs turn red. We sipped a little wine. Neither of us drink very much anymore, usually just a little wine. By midnight I was giggly. We snuggled up in the old wood bed. It had a beautiful wedding ring quilt on it, and it was nice and warm. This was one of the best nights I have ever had. I feel that we are bonded for life now.

David woke early, before sunrise, and he woke me just as the sun showed its face above the horizon. We went out on the porch steps and sat and enjoyed the quietness of the glistening dew and the sun slowly inching its way into view, the sky turning pink, red, and then bright gold. It was breathtaking, and we got the urge to make passionate love right there on the steps with the sun smiling upon us. The air had a nice feel. It was cool and refreshing brushing against our bodies, and it made our lovemaking even more erotic.

After we made love, we went back inside and cooked breakfast together. We ate, dressed, and then took a walk in the woods. It was so peaceful, almost as if we were walking on the edge of the universe.

Saturday evening we both did some reading, and I wrote some poems. Later we played chess. After that, I read this poem to David. It's one I wrote for him.

The Things We Share

The things we share
Are precious and rare
I can't think of anything I'd rather do
Than spend my time with you
It's funny but it's true
I could spend my time
   just looking at you

I could listen to your happy laughter
   the day long
I could taste those sweet lips for eons
I could sniff your erotic aroma
   season after season
I could make love to you forever
   without rhyme or reason
You are in control, you got me overwhelmed
And you know what? I don't give a damn

When we talk it's not conversation
But more like an orchestra
  in harmony with nature
That sets the tone for spirited elation
When we dance it's not just a step or a beat
But more like two bodies dancing
  with one set of feet
When you move I move, it's never too soon
It's like we become the music
  or the rhythm in the tune
When we are on the water and it's twilight
The stars sprinkled about and shining bright
The moon is a bold, big round pearl
  looking down on us
It is peaceful, serene, nothing or no one
  making a fuss
I lay my head on your chest
  and look up at you
Then rub your nose
Like the Eskimos do
If this ain't heaven what can it be?
Because to me the things we share
  are definitely heavenly.

He smiled after I read the poem. It was great not to have a television, or a radio, or a telephone. There was no trace of civilization here.

At dark we sat out and watched the stars come out one by one. We could see them twinkle, and soon a whole, wide sky full of stars opened up for us. We talked about buying a telescope. We talked about whether or not there's life on other planets, in other galaxies. We couldn't stop talking and laughing. We talked about Merci. David admitted that he seldom takes time off to do this sort of thing. But he said he needed the space, and since I needed the space too, why not get away together?

I told him some of the gossip floating around Merci. He assured me that gossip is a pastime at the hospital and that I didn't need to get involved with it. We did talk some about the doctor who murdered his wife, and then we talked about Freda. David said that some of the hostility also stemmed from the fact that the director of social services was partial to a certain home health agency, called Happy Days Care. It was even rumored among top officials that she was taking payoffs from this agency. Anyway, Freda disagreed with the director's choice of agencies, because she was extremely partial to a black agency called Maid For Care. The two agencies became competitive, and the owner of Happy Days Care encouraged the social service director to fire Freda, which is what she did. But of course, that didn't work, and the rest is history. Apparently the only reason the director is still there is because no one can prove she's taking payoffs.

On Sunday evening, we packed up and went back to the city. I felt sad in a way to return to this hustle and bustle. When we got to my house, David asked me to tell him two things I've always wanted to do but couldn't because I didn't have the money. I thought about it and said that 1) I would love to shop 'til I drop, and 2) I would love to go to Las Vegas.

November 13
Saturday, Midnight

I'm awfully tired because I moved today. Yes, I finally relocated to Hill Terrace Apartments. I left the old apartment behind, and I really like it here. There's a recreational room that can be used for parties. There's also a swimming pool and tennis court. It's very nice. Georgia would really like this apartment.

November 18
Thursday, 10:00 P.M.

I got an invitation from Rachel today, the woman I went to college with who's now working wonders with her home for handicapped children. Anyway, she's invited me and my guest to a Kwanzaa celebration. I have no earthly idea what this celebration is or what it means. The card said, "You are invited to Kwanzaa on November 27." The card also listed the Nguzo Saba Principles, the seven basic symbols and principles.

Umoja——Unity
Kujichagulia——Self determination
Ujima——Collective Work and Responsibility
Ujamma——Cooperative economics
Nia——Purpose
Kuumba——Creativity
Imani——Faith

Rachel had written her telephone number at the bottom of the card, so I called her. She was excited to hear from me. "Norma, Girl," she said, "I have been looking for you for months, and I finally saw Georgia, and she gave me your new address. I just couldn't have Kwanzaa and not invite you! After all, Girl, you gave me a reason to live. I mean, I would have never thought about starting a home for handicapped children. You know, it's the most important thing I've ever done. Anyway, Norma, lately I've really been into black history, and I've been teaching it to the children." She rattled on for twenty minutes. I asked her what was Kwanzaa exactly, and she explained that it's a gathering of friends, relatives, and acquaintances, where everyone comes together for fellowship and to celebrate. I asked her if I could bring some other people, and she said that of course I could. So I invited David, Georgia, Valerie and Jack, Jewel, and Carmen.

I also asked Rachel to explain these Nguzo Saba Principles. She said that following these principles will make for a better, more stable, harmonious way of life. She said I could learn more about them at the Kwanzaa celebration. Then she suggested that I might even be interested in taking some black history classes.

November 28
Sunday, 6:00 P.M.

The Kwanzaa celebration was so nice. Practically everyone there was dressed in African costume, except for me and my guests. It was good seeing Rachel. She just glows. Everything that girl touches these days is turning to gold. She just got a big federal grant to help her run her program. She's really into black history now. As a matter of fact, Rachel is going to Africa in the spring. She got another grant to pay for it. She even got me and David excited about the black history classes, so we signed up to take some. Georgia and Valerie seemed interested too, and even Carmen said she would take the classes. And as for Jewel, well, she could probably teach a class herself. She already knew all about the seven principles.

I feel really good, like God is blessing me.

Chapter Twelve: December

December 6
Monday, 7:00 P.M.

David and I started the black history classes at Matthew Zion Baptist Church. They're taught on Mondays and Wednesdays, and they're free to anyone that wants to learn. There were even some white people in class. I learned more about the seven principles of blackness, and I learned about people I'd never even heard of before now. Like Bill Pickett, for instance, a black man who created the art of bulldozing, or steer wrestling. Need a teaspoon of sugar in your coffee? A black American made it possible. Is a blood transfusion needed to save a life? A black American made that possible, too. Now, David has gone overboard. He went out and bought all kinds of books and maps. But it *is* interesting to learn about the different customs in various parts of Africa. I'm glad that I'm expanding my horizons.

December 18
Saturday, 10:00 P.M.

David called me early this morning, around 7:00. He said he had a surprise for me. So I got dressed, and he was here by 8:30.

He wouldn't tell me where we were going, even though I kept asking. We stopped at a restaurant and had breakfast, and he kept looking at his watch. At 9:30, we got back into his car, and he turned on the radio, which was odd, because he usually plays tapes. We were talking, and I wasn't paying much attention, and then I heard it, and I asked David if I'd heard the D.J. on the radio correctly. Had he said what I think he'd said? David nodded. Then the D.J. repeated it. "This is for Norma Jean Harris from David Monroe. I love you, and this day is declared Norma Jean Harris Day." That's what I love so much about David—he's always so exciting. I can never tell what he's going to do next. I grinned like crazy. No one has ever declared a holiday for me before. We drove downtown, and David parked. He looked at me, grinned, and said, "Hell, I must love you, since I'm going to stay with you today while you shop 'til you drop."

"What?" I asked.

He said, "You heard me. I want you to shop 'til you drop." I wanted to pinch myself, because I couldn't believe it was real. But sure enough, we got out of the car, walked slowly to the stores, and at first we just window shopped, and then we went in. I tried on clothes, shoes, everything. I bought some Christmas gifts, too. I got a nice suit for Mama and even something for my friends. David said, "You know, that is what I love about you. You're always thinking of others. I give you a shopping trip, and you buy things for others." Yes, and I even bought something for David.

Then he said, "I really hate to tell you this." My heart started to pound—I had the sudden thought that this had all been a prank. He looked really serious and said, "While you're shopping, you'd better buy something that'll be comfortable to wear in the desert." I looked at him like a fool. I could not imagine what he was talking about. He said, "Well, you were the one that wanted to go to Las Vegas." I said I needed to sit down. He kept talking. "New Year's Eve is my birthday, and I want to celebrate it with you in Las Vegas. Now, we'll probably go to a couple of shows while we're there, so buy something for that, and buy some of those cute silk teddies—not that you'll wear them for long." I felt like he was Santa Claus. I can't remember when I have felt so good. I'm going to continue to wear my rainbow crystal bracelet.

I shopped 'til I dropped. My feet were swollen, and my arms were tired from carrying so many packages. I spent over $2,000, and since I'm a bargain shopper, I had a hell of a lot of stuff.

December 20
Monday, 7:30 P.M.

Some shit went down at work today that I did not like. First of all, some of the women that I have met are jealous as hell of me, especially since David had the D.J. broadcast his love for me. One of the nurses that works in surgery said to me, "I see you are another link in the chain of fools for David Monroe." And a nurse in medicine, a very pretty girl, came up to me and said aggressively, "You should leave David Monroe alone. He is mine." Her name was Cynthia Parker. I made it a point to get some information on her, and I found out that she had dated David for about a year. This was a few years ago, and when things didn't work out, she had trouble adjusting. I heard she even had an abortion after David told her under no circumstances was he going to marry her. All this shit pissed me off. I did *not* want to get into a relationship with another womanizing man. I mean, Mark was enough for a lifetime.

David is so sweet. It's hard to believe this shit. I called him, and he could tell I was not in a good mood. He agreed to meet me at my apartment around 6:00. David had never seen me angry. By the time we met, I was calmer but still irritated. I told him what happened.

He said they were just jealous. "Norma, look, I told you I haven't been an angel all these years. It's just been in the past five years that I've been getting my act together. As for Cynthia having an abortion, yes, that's true. But Norma, Cynthia tricked me. She told me she was on the pill, but she was trying to get pregnant because she wanted money from me. In fact, on our very first date, she even asked me to buy her a Gucci watch. I just didn't like it. I didn't want to marry her, and I wasn't going to marry her. I did *not* say I wouldn't take care of the child. But she decided she wouldn't have the baby, because the pregnancy obviously wasn't going to accomplish what she wanted it to. I washed my hands of her then. Now, I have been honest with you. I'd really be a fool to have the D.J. announce to the world that you're my lady if I had ties with any of those women at Merci." I knew he was right, so I let it go. I rubbed his nose Eskimo-style, and sparks started to fly.

December 26
Sunday, 8:00 P.M.

We visited with my mother on Christmas, and she had everything nicely decorated with Christmas lights, even outside in the hedges. Mama cooked a delicious meal. I mean, I'm not bragging, but Mama can burn when she wants to. Anyway, I could tell Mama liked David, and I could tell he liked her. They seemed to hit it off from the beginning, and they talked like they were old friends. Mama loved her suit and the pearl necklace and earrings I got her. She even said she would probably wear the outfit to church next Sunday.

David in his loving, cunning way pulled all my adolescent secrets out of my mother. I mean, she just played right into his hands. She told him about every boyfriend I ever had. She also told him about my singing days with the church choir, about how I used to partici- pate in talent shows, and about how I won prizes for singing and for writing and reciting poetry. She showed him picture albums I had not seen in years. As a matter of fact, I'd forgotten about them. Now he knows how everybody in this family looks, where they live, the kind of work they do, and what kind of personality they have. When we left, he had a damn good idea who Norma Jean Harris was and is. When I got home, there was a beautiful basket of expensive cologne, perfume, body cream and powder, some gorgeous lingerie, and a dozen long-stemmed red roses waiting for me. David is spoiling me rotten. I gave him the poem I wrote for him, "The Things We Share." I had it embroidered and framed, and I wrote another one for his birthday and had it mounted on wood. I love him, I can't do enough for him, and he is so giving to me. I don't ask for anything, but I get everything I want and more. But you know, I would love him even if he didn't have the money. I really and truly believe that he cares about me and my happiness, and I love him for that.

December 31
Friday, 11:00 A.M.

David and I left Knoxville for Chicago on a 6:30 flight yesterday evening. David had a sudden change in his schedule, and we had to go to Chicago first before going on to Las Vegas. He's the Chairman of the Board of a non-profit organization there, and they called a meeting suddenly. It was okay with me because I've never been to Chicago. It was a smooth flight, and when we approached the city I looked out my window, and all the brilliant lights looked like a giant chandelier. I can see why songs have been written about Chicago. It was very cold at the airport, and I didn't have my thick, warm winter coat. My face was burning with cold as we stood out front, waiting for a taxi. We're staying at one of the largest hotels in the city, and it's very elegant. The downtown area is beautifully decorated for Christmas. David was in meetings most of yesterday and will be again for half of today. He gave me money to go sightseeing and shopping, so I went to Marshall Fields, the Watertower, and all along the Magnificent

Mile. I was impressed with the fact that Chicago has some of the world's most prosperous businesses. This place is so alive, even though the weather is so cold. I saw a guy dressed like Santa playing the drums on the street, and there was a group of young boys out dancing for money. I don't feel this kind of excitement or see this kind of talent on the streets at home.

January 1
Saturday, 2:00 A.M.

Downtown Chicago is gorgeous at night, especially from a horse and buggy. It was so romantic. We held hands during the entire ride and rubbed noses to keep warm.

Now, David's in bed, and he has a smile on his face. I can't wait until tomorrow. First of all, I have a good idea I want to try out. It's about a mentorship program we can set up with some of the inner city black youth back home. My plan is to start out working with the young men, then start a program for young women, too. David will like this idea. I hope so, anyway, because I'm going to ask him to be a mentor and a financial donor. I have a job for Georgia, too. She can be the volunteer recruiter, because that girl knows everybody, and the people she doesn't know, she knows something about. Valerie can be a counselor, because she has children and she really relates very well to them. Her husband, Jack, will make a great mentor. Carmen will make a great counselor, especially since she's beaten the odds and carved out a career for herself and is now planning to get off welfare. Jewel can teach black history classes, and Rachel can be a consultant. I will be the project director, and there you have it—a job for everyone. All this stuff is going around and around in my head. I know it will work, and I'm excited about it.

David said something about us leaving from here and going on to Las Vegas, then maybe on to Reno. Can you imagine what that means? I can't wait until tomorrow.

144

As I reflect on the past year, I realize that it posed a challenge for me in every way—physically, mentally, emotionally, spiritually, and financially. I've been constantly dealing with change and adversity. I cannot recall having had another year with so many obstacles and unfortunate situations and circumstances. But at the same time, I cannot recall a year in which I experienced so much personal growth. I know one thing—I'm glad I didn't give up on life. I'm glad I didn't give up on men, and most of all, I'm glad I didn't give up on me. And something else—I thank God for my family and my friends, because I could not have made it through this year without them.

Life is a learning experience, a process of daily decision-making. I suppose what we should always keep in mind is that what we do today will affect us in some way tomorrow. Life isn't a dress rehearsal. It's for real, and it's the only life we have. No matter what happens, I intend to give it everything I've got. Starting right now, I am so full of anticipation that I can hardly wait until tomorrow.